CHATTERING

Stories

LOUISE STERN

GRANTA

Granta Publications, 12 Addison Avenue, London W11 4QR

First published in Great Britain by Granta Books 2010
This paperback edition published by Granta Books 2011

A CIP catalogue record for this book is available
from the British Library.

1 3 5 7 9 10 8 6 4 2

ISBN 978 1 84708 177 3

Printed and bound in Great Britain by
CPI Bookmarque, Croydon CR0 4TD

Louise Stern grew up in Fremont, California, and is the fourth generation of her family to be born deaf. She moved to London in 2002, where she is an artist and the founder of *Maurice*, a contemporary art magazine for children. This is her first book.

More praise for *Chattering*:

'Stern is a remarkably gifted writer and this is a superb collection of stories. Stern writes in a wonderfully sharp and vivid style and she knows how to tell a story with immense pace and charm' M. J. Hyland

'Louise Stern's stories really are good – taut and powerful and funny too' Tessa Hadley

'Louise Stern writes stories about young men and women on the edge, stories that stay in your head long after you have finished reading them . . . *Chattering* is utterly compelling and expresses what it is like to be deaf – especially when you're also young and reckless – in a way I have never read or understood before' *Observer*

'Wry, deceptively gauche, and gets better with each piece . . . Stern tackles wider issues of isolation in society, while her final tale, "The Deaf School", uncompromisingly addresses the life choices – or lack of them – available to the hearing impaired' *Guardian*

'An intriguing, insightful and refreshing debut collection of short stories' *Big Issue*

'Reading an accurately rendered account of a signed conversation was a bit of a revelatory trip for us, and one we would recommend to anyone' *Dazed & Confused*

'Stern's observations are ruthlessly sharp and curiously revealing about the lives of the hearing' *The Times*

'Stern writes in a style that is predominantly clear and concise . . . the characters and situations stay with you, even as you know their lives are moving on elsewhere. There is very little dialogue, but lots of internal monologue and precise visual observations that convey people's presences in a way I've never read before. It's clear that being a native signer has allowed Stern to offer a perspective that is both piercingly insightful and startlingly new' *Irish Times*

'Intense without ever being extravagant . . . In one of the best pieces, "Window Washer", Stern shows talent in stuffing so much insight – wit, refusal, isolation, economics – into a single unassuming exchange' *Sunday Times*

'Exactly what I want of fiction – I want it to take me places I couldn't get to myself' Tracy Chevalier, *Daily Telegraph*

'A stunning debut, each tale painting a delicate picture of a deaf life . . . In telling us about deaf people rarely featured in print, Stern not only gives them a voice, but reveals herself as a writer of extraordinary promise. Recommended' *One in Seven*

'Set all over the globe from London to LA, Brazil to the Caribbean, the twelve tales are told in a lucid, deceptively simple style that allows Stern to make unsettling and bizarre situations seem close to mundane – and vice versa . . . There is more than enough here to enjoy. Understated and quietly disturbing, Stern's is a new literary voice we should be listening to' *Pen Pusher*

CONTENTS

RIO

In Rio the velvety air felt easy and comfortable. We slept on Copacabana beach and our sandals were stolen by one of the bony, dark-skinned group in rags who had set up camp under the nearby palm trees ringed by bits of rubbish. In the night, after we felt in the sand by our heads for the rubber sandals and discovered them gone, Eva strode over, pointed at some of the boys and then pointed at her foot.

—Give me back, she gestured. You give me back.

She banged her fist against one hand.

—Me fight you. Come on. Give me back. Me fight you.

One of the ragged, wily ones gave her our sandals. Her back seemed very straight next to theirs.

One night we were drunk on the main boardwalk on lemony cold caipirinhas in plastic cups when a man walking by gave us some shells with the date and Copacabana scrawled on them in black Sharpie marker. He was white and had shrivelled calves covered with sunspots. Pale strands of hair hung off them. His eyes

3

were like a rodent's – hungry and lusty and unashamed that he would eat whatever he could find, but they were not malicious. He handed over the broken shells as if they were rosaries.

I was sitting on the wall between the beach and the street watching Eva. Unusually, she was drunker than I was. Some of the Brazilian law students we had met a few nights before were there that night.

—You crazy, she signed to them, pointing to them. One finger was going in circles beside her head. She laughed.

We always wondered at her laughter, how people invariably looked at us, startled, when she laughed. Some childhood friends of hers had told her that her laugh sounded like a horse's neigh, and she had been self-conscious about it since then. I could hear more than she could and told her that it didn't sound like a horse, but I couldn't hear well enough to know exactly what it did sound like, and nobody else would give a satisfying description. They just stared, and we never really felt we had any kind of handle on what was behind their bewilderment.

Sometimes now I thought it was more bemusement, but whatever it was, it frustrated me to the point of tears. People would call it a pure sound, and we wondered if it was only pure because we couldn't hear it. It was like an imaginary friend that everyone could see except for you, who insisted on attaching itself to you with gooey suction lips, and who everyone liked better than they liked you. It frustrated Eva even more, though. In her mind the horse's neigh had turned into a donkey's bray, spit flying everywhere through yellowed teeth like a whale's baleen.

The rodent man was attracted to her laugh. I saw it in his eyes as he looked at her, but then he scuttled away. I wondered at it for a minute – he seemed to me the kind to want a closer sniff at least. He was the kind to be attracted to shiny bits of broken glass, to want to grab them all up and hoard them in a box.

But then later, when I went across the street to have a piss in the restaurant loo, there he was at a table, watching Eva through binoculars. He was delighted that I had seen him at it. On the paper covering the table he started scribbling, telling me who he was, where he had been, who he had been with, trying to show me the pieces of glass in his box. He had collected a lot. I saw him look at me sideways when he thought I wasn't looking and he was grinning with sheer delight. He showed me a khaki canvas shoulder bag filled with broken shells like the ones he had given us earlier, and told me that he wandered Copacabana all day giving them out. He had other assorted trinkets in the bag, pads of paper and things that appeared to me either junk or esoteric fetishes, which he held up, tittering. He didn't really ask about us, just wanted to tell me who he was. He had been an executive at a paper company, now retired and become beach bum.

Eva had come over to the restaurant by that time and was hopping and skipping from table to table. The Brazilian law students had ended up at one table. At another was the huge black man with his heavy gold chains.

With her strong rounded arms that always appeared to me to be a bit masculine in a pleasing way, Eva would tell me again and again how the thickest of his chains swayed into the air when he bent over to write to us on the night we'd first met him. The big gold cross on the end of it swung under our eyes. The way Eva signed it, the cross stayed in the air for a long, emphatic moment, swaying back and forth just a bit but always staying for a few seconds more at the height of its trajectory. That was how we remembered him, because that moment had been re-enacted over and over again, her fingers becoming that shiny huge cross hanging there longer than it should have. We loved it. Now he was here in the restaurant with all the others.

They were all talking, chattering over me. As a child I had longed to be able to overhear. Not any more, usually.

The girl on the right turned to me.

—Oh, you hear not . . . she gestured. She held two fingers up to her mouth, miming drinking from a bottle.

—Me drink, drink, drink. Her head was thrown back and her eyes closed, the throat in outline. Her skin had yellowish pores. Her hand, with its index finger and thumb extended, went up and down into her mouth again and again.

—Drink, drink, drink. One finger went down one cheek, and then the other.

—Me cry, cry, cry. Cry, cry, cry. Then she turned away and slid effortlessly into animated conversation with the black man.

I wondered exactly where this sorrow she had just told me about was stored in her body, where she held it that she could call it up so fast and then dispose of it so fast. I wondered if it was because she could speak that she knew how to deposit the sorrow outside herself so efficiently. That was the part I envied.

The rodent man came to the table. His eyes were brighter than before. He had caught the fever. He had a plan now and he was eager to tell us, but only if we went with him somewhere. It was a place for us to stay. We had no place to sleep anyway and had planned to sleep on Copacabana next to the same people who had stolen our sandals and who were now cautious, frightened by us.

I liked this man well enough; he had already shown me all of his bits of glass, the shiny magpie collection of his mind, and I felt comfortable with it.

—Okay we will go with you, I told him.

—You stay here, I get car, come back for you, he mimed.

Eva was drunker and drunker, flitting around the

restaurant, so it suited me fine to stay there and wait for him and let her play it out.

She was passed out flat on the pavement in front of the restaurant when he returned for us in a gleaming black executive car. He had showered and was neatly dressed in a pale blue button-down shirt with long sleeves and black stiff pants, the opposite of the dishevelled beach bum we had first met. I sat next to him in the car with Eva sprawled on the back seat asleep.

After an hour's drive through the dark warm streets, we came up to a set of imposing gates that matched the car. There was a mansion behind them, but it had an odd feel to it, not quite a house, not quite a hotel, but not quite anything else either. It was square and stolid like one of the more expensive chain hotels in the States, but with a tattiness to it that I had never seen in any hotel. A sign next to it read 'Panda'.

At the moment the car paused beside the Panda sign ready to go down the ramp into the concrete parking garage, Eva woke up and was overcome by the sight. She'd always had limpid fantasies of sex and luxury and our surroundings were a good backdrop for them.

The garage was lit with fluorescent strip lights. The parking spaces were precisely marked out, two for each of the small doors that were set at regular intervals around the walls. It felt as if we were in a Super 8 motel. I wondered what this place really was.

Up a narrow flight of steps was a nice-sized but

unremarkable room like one in a pricey but far from beautiful airport hotel. It had the same beige wallpaper with thin brown pinstripes and the same black nubbly carpet that those places have. But the main room had a mirror on the ceiling and a wall-mounted television. The rodent man turned on the television to show us that it played only porn. It was American porn, starring platinum-blonde lovelies. There was a waterbed in the centre of the room with a stiff red velvet cover. Off the main room was a white-tiled bathroom taken up almost entirely by a jacuzzi. On the wall in the bathroom above the his-and-hers sinks was one of those theatrical make-up mirrors with round light bulbs all around the top and the sides.

—You two stay here, me come back for you in the morning, he mimed to me.

Eva and I slithered around naked in the hot tub for a while after he left, gossiping and giggling in the bubbles, and then we jumped on the waterbed. We turned off the television and made faces to ourselves in the ceiling mirror.

In the morning a maid brought us a huge spread of a breakfast. There were fried eggs with runny rich yolks and Brazilian bread, sweet pineapple and mango slices, strong coffee, tomatoes and cucumber wedges, creamy butter, and fresh-squeezed juices. It was delicious and we finished it all up.

Soon the man came back and took us to a small dark

café by the beach with wooden tables and benches, where we had more coffee. He told us it was the same café where the famous song 'The Girl from Ipanema' had been written.

He had brought a yellow lined pad to scribble to us on.

'Men always want silent women,' he said. 'You two are the perfect women. You are beautiful and no words come out of you to ruin the fantasy, and you can never hear the filth that is said around you. Completely untouched, untouchable. Men would pay anything you wanted, to be with you. I will introduce you to some.'

—What you got to offer us? I said with a tough cheekiness that surprised me. We do it without you.

Eva laughed nervously and met my eyes, but of course neither of us wanted to do without the safety of the rodent man.

We would be Marina and Kristina. He had a special affection for these schoolgirl names. We needed the appropriate costumes, he said. We went shopping in small boutiques with bright jewelled chandeliers. The other shoppers were the slender wives of Brazilian businessmen, the kind of rich women who always had a hard, crystallized certainty that I envied.

Eva and I chose two tops – a small zebra-print tube that only covered our breasts, and another tight purple tie-dye top with 'Olá' written across the front that made us laugh. The rodent man vetoed a whorish pair of clear plastic stilettos that we wanted, to our disappointment. He told us to meet him that night in a café we knew along the Copacabana beach.

The evening was like the other evenings we would spend with him in cafés in Rio, dressed in our costumes. At the end of each evening, he always told us when and where we would meet the next time. Sometimes we would meet two or three nights in a row. Other times we wouldn't see him for three days before he reappeared. He always pointed out potential clients, mostly large businessmen with soft pouches under their necks and starched shirts. We dismissed each one for some made-up reason, or quoted an outrageously high price for our services. One night I showed him a slip of crumpled-up paper with a telephone number on it, writing to him that the number belonged to a potential client and that I would be sure to bring him in when fee negotiations reached the crucial stage. His eyes brightened and he had that rodent look again.

After a few nights Eva and I wondered whether he actually wanted to close the deal with anyone, or whether sharing these possibilities with us was all he wanted, nothing else.

During the day, if we hadn't met anyone interesting, we would wander around, eat, sneak into the pools at the fancier hotels, laze around on the beach. We slept on Copacabana beach or at the house or apartment of whoever we'd met that day. The rodent man had asked us if we wanted to take up residence in the Panda, and it was tempting, but we didn't like the idea of him always knowing where we were. Besides the Panda seemed to us a slightly boring place to stay for more than one night. We never had problems finding a place to sleep. A taxi driver took us to stay with his family in a *favela*, where we slept on the floor in the middle of the children's room, surrounded by five painted metal bunk beds. We stayed up watching soccer on a television set on top of a plastic orange crate in the street with everyone in the neighbourhood crowded around, jumping up and down when Rio scored.

Another night we stayed in a homeless shelter with a Brazilian Indian woman whose short hair curled around her generous face. Long lines spread from the outer corners of her eyes. We sat with her all day on the boardwalk behind the square of blue felt she used to display the cheap beaded jewellery she sold. The crack she also sold she kept safely in the front pocket of her long skirt. The night after, we stayed in the best hotel in Rio, with a glaringly white-toothed music producer from LA we'd met when we snuck into the pool area of his hotel. In our string bikinis – Eva's was navy blue and mine tomato red – we looked like any other tourists, even though we had been living on the streets for months by then and hadn't showered for a few days. The chlorinated water of the pool was shower enough. The producer wanted to party and talk. And the day after that we had been asked by the rodent man to meet him in the early afternoon. He'd asked us to meet him on a street corner in one of the better neighbourhoods. Was it a visit to a possible client? I was a bit excited by this idea, but at the same time, I didn't want to meet a client in their home, in their territory, with their things and their own smell around them. The reality of it, whichever way it actually lay, would have more of a chance to take over then.

This time he was dressed in neat khaki shorts and a mauve T-shirt. He took us up a wide white staircase into a clean, spacious apartment with dark polished wooden floors and French windows along one wall, looking onto the trees outside. A woman with a soft body and grey-streaked hair got up from the flowered sofa to come over to us, and a young girl walked into the room.

On his yellow pad, the rodent man wrote to us in a few fragmented words that this was his wife and daughter. Turning to them, he started talking, his mouth opening and closing, the thin wrinkled upper lip pressing tightly against the slightly fleshier lower lip. It was in Portuguese, so I didn't even have a chance to catch a word or two on his lips, and I was thankful that I didn't. He gestured towards us a few times, explaining us to them. Later we were served Earl Grey tea and Brazilian cake on a tray before leaving.

We met him at a café in the evening, again dressed in our costumes, but there was a new and strange feeling of something closing in, a possibility of knowing exactly what it was that this man wanted from us, and I didn't like it . . . And it had become boring to keep these assignations with him night after night. So one night we stood him up and never went back.

A few weeks later, we saw the rodent man on the boardwalk in the middle of the carnival festivities. He was wearing a sign on his front with some words in Portuguese scrawled across it. Some people near us told us that the words meant 'I'm a Lesbian'. His eyes were fogged over and he didn't recognize us.

He was the only one who said it. I know, even if I often don't want to believe it, that it is true what he said about the specific quality of our silence. It is potential and remains only potential. It is like water, the liquid clear and thin, something you can feel but not hold down in any way. That is the silence that surrounds me and Eva always.

ROADRUNNER

In the front of the eighteen-wheeler she sat next to the truck driver who called himself the Roadrunner. He had a greenish tattoo of a roadrunner on his forearm. His driving partner the Cat slept in the bunk above the cab. The Roadrunner was telling his life story in a few short gestures.

—Wife left and I am alone now, he said by miming a wedding ring coming off his finger. Then he had wept and drunk. That was all he said, and maybe all that he could say to her. Because she could not hear him and she shared no other language with him.

He asked almost half-heartedly for a fuck by pulling one finger in and out of a hole made by circling the fingers on his other hand. She told him with a ring made of thumb and forefinger that she was married, that her husband was at home. He seemed satisfied with this, as if he had only asked because it was somehow the thing he thought a man should do if he found himself alone with a girl.

He also said that the Cat, asleep upstairs, was a serial

shagger, giving her a short mime of the way the body of the Cat moved in the act, outlining the curves of a woman with his stocky, hard palms. Content with this, he turned back to the road, his eyes firm on it, and seeming to forget about her next to him. He drank beer after beer, rolling down the window to throw out the empty cans that rolled harmlessly down to join the trash along the sides of the road.

They were working their way down the Mexican coast, the Roadrunner to deliver his truckload of whatever he was carrying, and the girl to catch another ride. She didn't really have a plan, just wanted to see how far she could take herself and to find out how soon she would feel compelled to go back home. But the strange world she had left felt very far away, and it got even further away with every day she hitchhiked.

It was the world of the deaf, a small, fierce encampment in the middle of hearing people who talked and talked all the time, their mouths opening and closing endlessly. She had hated it growing up, so many things about it. How claustrophobic everything felt, the people working at the deaf school being the same people at the parties her parents threw and their children being her classmates. She had hated not being able to communicate with anyone else outside that tiny cluster of people. She loved the solid language that the deaf shared, but she longed for the smooth subtleties in the books she read constantly, the subtleties she was sure hearing people knew how to give to one another. Walking the streets of the suburb she had grown up in, she would watch people walking past her and know that she would not be able to say anything to them nor they to her.

Her school was next to the school for the retards. On the small yellow buses that picked up the deaf kids and the retarded kids from their homes to take them to their schools, the retards lolled on their seats, their necks sagging so that their heads hung low. They usually had open mouths. Sometimes their noses bled and she watched, disgusted. They didn't really know their noses were bleeding. She sat behind them, watching them bang their heads against the hard brown vinyl of the seats with a regular, obstinate rhythm and watching the people outside look into the buses at them and at her.

On days out the deaf kids walked in lines behind the hearing teachers. The hearing teachers occupied themselves by telling the deaf kids to behave, because if they didn't people would think deaf people were all retarded as well. The hearing teachers' bodies were stupid and heavy. When they signed, their movements didn't have the same grace as those of the deaf people, yet they didn't recognize this obvious difference. The teachers said, accusingly and knowingly, with a look of smugness, 'Do you want people to think you're animals?'

When she became a teen, hearing people paid attention to her. The hearing boys came to the house, but she always felt intimidated by all the things she could never say to them and by all the things she imagined they had to say urgently to her that they would not be able to. Now, out in the truck, it seemed to her that it was much easier this way, this silence with the Roadrunner. Maybe better, even. By that time she'd had more chance to talk to hearing people and was slightly more confident. But talking to them left her even more hungry - it was like an addiction that could never be satisfied, always clinging on to the delusion that the next word, the next conversation, the next person would be the time when she would find a way to make her words flow without suffocating her idea of this person, squeezing the air out of it.

But their words squirted and dashed away so quickly, and pushed her further and further away from any sense of them. In the morning after a party she would reread a conversation she'd had and wonder what it meant – what remained of it in the daylight, what was solid – in a way she never had to wonder when she talked to people in sign language. It wasn't because deaf people were better people or more honest, it was just because she could hold on to the solidity of their language.

She still didn't know how to hold on to written language outside of books. She didn't know how to explain herself in it so that she was sure of whatever it was she had said when the other person left the conversation.

She was mostly happy in her body and with the way it felt when she moved around, and she was happy in the refuge in her head, if some torture or some boy didn't crowd it. When she met other people she was mostly happy being next to them and with the moments when their eyes met in understanding. But trying to communicate brought her misery.

Sitting next to the Roadrunner in the truck, she thought back to the time, growing up, when she realized she had no chance of communicating with anyone around her. Now, she thought she might like it, just being on her own.

She glanced over at him in the seat next to her. Fat and jowly, with hard small brown hands, but again she noticed and liked how firm his eyes were on the road. She wondered how she could understand who he really was in just this time spent together. Even if they could communicate, she didn't think that was the way. The large square of light that came in from the living room and framed itself above her sister's bed, a thin line of shade dividing the square unevenly in two, was the thing she remembered most about her childhood bedroom. It was the most intimate memory she could call up, the steady accompaniment to all her night-time terrors. It seemed to her – she wasn't sure exactly why – that once she had seen what pattern of light on the wall he was accustomed to seeing in the night, she could slip into his life without knowing that much about him or about it, and then slip out of his life again when she felt the urge.

But the urge was so thin, both towards him and away from him. She felt that she would feel the same for almost anyone she met, and that she could be content next to nearly anyone, as long as she didn't know what they were saying. Or maybe she just told herself that. She didn't know.

The Roadrunner was tapping her on the shoulder.

—You eat? he gestured to her. Drink?

He was turning off the road and into a service station. She swung her leg out of the truck and onto the metal step, and then with a large jump down to the concrete, she followed him into the station. It was funny, seeing him under the fluorescent lights, out of the warm small truck cab. His body looked different when he was standing up, more squat, his lower half thick and clumsy. She felt guilty and somewhat disloyal observing this. Next to the other people in the service station he was lost to her again. They got some greasy burritos and another six-pack of Corona.

Back in the truck, the desert landscape spread out around them. It went on and on all the way out to the mountains, flat and quiet and massive, and she felt comfortable being silent in the midst of a panorama that was so content in its own silence. When the city was silent, you could always feel the noise squished up in its hiding places, tensed with energy, ready to jump out again. She loved the city, but it made her feel strangely and pathetically apologetic sometimes, because she had no noise of her own to match it with.

They ate and drank side by side in the truck, watching the road go by and the lights of the small towns and the occasional big city get larger, and then smaller again behind them. They drove for days – mostly the Roadrunner did the driving, but sometimes the Cat drove too.

It was much the same with her and the Cat as it was with her and the Roadrunner. The Cat was taller, leaner, darker, younger and more energetic. He laughed more, made more jokes. When he threw his beer out of the window he would tap her on the shoulder and point at the bottle rolling down to the trash heaps, giggling. She would giggle with him. He seemed to enjoy the idea of his mess joining all the rest of it. Sometimes he would poke her in the tummy, trying to tickle her, or he would slide against her on the truck seat when he sat up front with her while the Roadrunner was driving. But he still wasn't aggressive with her, or demanding of anything. She would buy food and beer for all of them when they stopped, and they seemed to appreciate the gesture.

Neither of them asked her to teach them any sign language. They seemed to feel that they could say to her all of what they needed to – Eat, Sleep, Fuck. What time is it? Are you married? Do you have kids? Where you go?

She felt fine. It was only when they stopped at a bar

for drinks with other truck drivers that she felt lonely and somewhat foolish for allowing herself to get into this situation. Under the suspicious eyes of the other truck drivers, she felt how fragile her position was, how easily the Roadrunner and the Cat could overpower her. She would sit by herself, smiling at the people around her and looking at the Roadrunner and the Cat talking to their friends. Paranoia overcame her a few times, and she thought she saw a change in their eyes. But once they were back in the truck it all faded away again.

One night they stopped in a small town outside of Guadalajara, where the Cat had friends. They told her with a few gestures that there was going to be a party, and she was excited. She wore a skirt and a shirt that had lain neatly folded at the bottom of her backpack, beneath all the shorts and vests she had been wearing every day. The skirt was silky polyester, a deep orange, and it waved smoothly against her tanned, dirty skin.

The room was filled with men, lounging on chairs pushed against the walls. Bright lights showed the dirt on the cracked floor. They were sipping beer from the bottle. They smiled slowly at her, and she felt uncomfortable.

There were a few women in the room, too, sitting by the men. Some met her eyes and then looked down quickly, without curiosity.

She leaned against the wall nearest to the door. The Cat put an arm around her waist, pulling her over to be introduced to some people. She allowed him to lead her towards one of them, a man older than the Cat but younger than the Roadrunner. A woman sat next to him. The man smiled broadly at her and she looked down at the floor, suddenly unsure about how she should meet his gaze. When she looked up, she saw that the woman by his side was staring at her.

The Cat elbowed her sharply, shaking his head; all the camaraderie of the days and nights in the truck, side by side in perfect symbiosis, had suddenly disappeared. He put his large hands on her shoulders and shook her quickly, briskly, impatiently.

She felt a huge tear, feeling the distance that was suddenly there. It was gone, the easiness between them. The Cat had no idea where she found herself in that moment, not being able to communicate with anyone there.

Tears spurted up violently in her eyes.

—Fuck you, she signed. Why you think me should be the one to understand you? You never ask me.

She pointed at him again and again. You, You, You, You, and pointed at herself again and again. Me, Me, Me, Me. It was simply a twist of the wrist that changed the sign from You to Me. No changing of the hand shape, no changing of anything except the direction the finger was pointing in. You never ask me.

The Cat looked at her and laughed, his big square yellow teeth showing.

'*No comprendo*,' she saw him say to his friends.

He brought a circled hand up to his mouth, asking if she wanted a drink, showing off the one thing he could say to her, the thing that she had thought insignificant next to everything else.

—Don't you know I don't understand anything you say either? she signed to him, the tears almost visible now. Don't you know you are as ridiculous to me as I am to you?

She turned around and went to the truck, stepped up on the high metal step, tugged the door open and got her backpack from the dusty floor of the cab. Jumping back down on to the soft tar of the parking lot, she saw the Roadrunner walking towards her.

—Bye, she waved to him.

She went and stood on the highway, thumb up.

BOAT

She had been flat hunting in London for months, lots of places. Most had linty carpet going up the stairs, and stains on the wall. You could cook from your bed in many of them. The idea of waking up, turning over, and stirring pots and pans while still in bed was funny, but in reality she didn't know if she could face it, the smells.

There was an ad in the paper one day for a room on a boat in Chelsea and she thought she'd go and see it for fun. Half of the houses on the road by the river were divided from the Chelsea streets by a brick wall, and on the corner was a pair of metal gates, propped open, leading to a brick walkway with neat beds of colourful flowers on both sides.

On the right of the walkway was another set of gates, these ones much more ornate and shiny, marking the way to an expanse of green grass. From the brick walkway, you had to cross over a small bridge leading onto a concrete jetty to get to the boat. There were metal cranes in the middle of the river, rusty and dripping with frayed ropes. A heron was perched on one skinny leg in the mud and sewage next to the cranes.

She stood watching the heron for a while. She was watching the river too.

A steep gangplank, painted forest green, led from the jetty to the boat. It wasn't a huge boat, but it looked sturdy and comfortable. The tide was low, so the boat was mired in the mud. Its hull was a pale yellow, dotted with round brass portholes, and above that was a square white cabin built on top of the hull. There were two decks; the main one had benches and potted geraniums at one end and coils of rope on the other, and from that deck was a ladder up the side of the cabin to the second deck. That one had a picnic table and chairs. There were empty beer bottles on the table and Christmas lights threaded around the railings.

Once down the gangplank, she walked around the coils of rope and found a wooden door at the side of the cabin. The living room had deep red walls, a huge red velvet sofa with shiny gold trim, and matching chairs next to it. A man was asleep on the sofa, a shimmery pool of saliva spreading on the pillow next to him. He must be the landlord, she thought, and sat down on one of the velvet chairs to wait for him to wake up.

After a long time watching him move various parts of himself around in his sleep, she thought she'd better wake him. He rubbed his nose and snorted and made grimaces before he opened his eyes. The coffee table was littered with empty bottles and overflowing ashtrays. She pointed a finger at her ear and shook her head, trying to tell him that she couldn't hear. He was confused, not finding himself here or there. With a paper and pen she told him that she was deaf and she was there about the room.

'No, I just met the guy who owns this boat last night at the pub,' he wrote. 'Can't remember his name. He's downstairs.'

He rolled over and fell back into sleep.

She was about to leave when a man came up the stairs from down below and entered the living room. He had a dingy white towel wrapped around his lower half and his bare chest was narrow and pale. He had thin freckled arms and an almost hysterical grin on his face. He did a little uncoordinated jig, his eyes unfocused. She told him she was deaf, and he wrote to her: 'Come live in the captain's room.'

So she did. The captain's room was at the bottom of the stairs, with built-in boxy cupboards for her clothes and portholes above the bed, and spider's webs at the farthest corners. Sometimes you could see the moon through one of the portholes. She would stare out of them for hours in the morning, or look at the water from the living-room windows.

It was fine living with the boat owner. During the daytime they would do their own thing. When he wasn't at work he sat in front of the television in the living room, staring blankly at whatever was on the screen, sometimes drinking beer. He told her he worked in the City, but she didn't really know what that meant. At the weekends he was either out partying, in a pub, or sleeping it off, staggering down to the kitchen for something to eat when he woke up in the early hours of the afternoon. She usually got up mid-morning or a bit later, depending on whether she had gone out or not.

He barely made contact with her, except to tell her to please wash her dishes or that she had made too much noise coming in the night before. She was on the boat more because she was working odd jobs and hours, trying to figure out what it was that she wanted to do. When they were both on the boat, she would sit on one of the red velvet chairs in her old jeans and boots and stare out at the water as he stared at the television. The boat swayed gently under them, sometimes rocking from side to side in the rain.

When she put on heels and make-up to go out to party with her friends or to go to dinner at a restaurant with a boyfriend, he would sometimes give her a more intense look than usual, but she could never decipher it.

Sometimes they would pass each other walking around the boat. There was always the same in-between kind of moment as when passing people in the corridor at work or on the narrow steps leading up from the Tube. The same nervous acknowledgement of the stranger you suddenly found to be physically very close to you, although these moments weren't happening in a public place but in the place where they both lived. In some ways she enjoyed the discomfort. It made home more interesting than just rooms to sleep and eat in. It was strange, this almost accidental close observation of the personal habits of someone you didn't really know. He liked beef samosas from the off-licence late at night, but he would always eat half and put the other half in the fridge for 'later' and then never eat the rest of it. And he used perfumed body wash and shampoo from a posh shop in Chelsea, which didn't fit with the rest of his habits.

Around six or seven in the evening the red wine would come out. After half a bottle the paper would come out, and he would start writing and writing to her. He wrote page after page without stopping, in small wriggly writing, telling her all kinds of things.

'We're all bottom feeders, like the skate and the ray,' he scribbled.

He would sit with his head in his hands, swaying, then look at her, his eyes unfocused, then get up and start dancing as if he were alone in the room, jumping around and waving his hands.

'Damn you Americans,' he would write.

She didn't know what exactly to say back to him.

In the morning, sober, they didn't look at each other.

Later in the evening, after a bottle or two, he often wrote that her silence had taught him so much.

'You and me, we're alike,' he would say. 'You understand me. Other people aren't like us.'

Mostly it seemed like he meant it. At times it made her very angry, with a hot rage deep down in herself, because she hadn't said much to him in between all that he said, or ever told him anything about what she was thinking or feeling. He didn't seem interested in that anyway. He didn't know her language. But there was something about the man, a quality that she recognized.

When he became angry because she didn't agree with what he said, he scared her. He would shout and shout at her, and she couldn't understand what it was that he was saying. His mouth gaped so far open and the insides of it looked so wet and so red, and the way he moved his thin body would become irregular. She would excuse herself and go to bed when that happened. She felt bad leaving him by himself in that state, but she couldn't stay.

He brought women back to the boat. When he wasn't around, they asked her how he felt about them. She didn't know what to say, as she had no idea what he felt about anything or if he even knew himself how he felt.

She would write to them, 'Sorry but I have no idea.'

In between the drinking sessions with him and going to work and everything else she would read, or think about how to explain this silence to other people. The silence was all around. Being on the boat, separated from the city, and having the water and space around them all the time made it harder to ignore. And the conversations with him brought it right to her nose. She felt all her words were petty pinpricks and didn't penetrate the state he was in or relay anything substantial to him. He felt close to her but far away, too. All the ways of getting across the silence that she could think of or that she sensed felt blasphemous, grimy, cheap reproductions, so she usually ended up looking out at the water instead. Sometimes she looked so long that the horizon, the line she could see between the flats on the other side of the river, disappeared. When you look so long at something it just goes away. She could momentarily feel something encompassing and comforting beyond that line, and then when she reached for it, the horizon appeared again.

The silence was nuanced, not blank and dead. It was mischievous and sly, and full of a sadness that managed not to be melancholy. She would laugh to herself when the silence tickled her, which was often.

She would try to clean the boat, to get rid of all the spider's webs in the corners of the portholes, the smelly cigarette butts in the many ashtrays and the wine-stained papers full of scribblings that would pile up on the bottom shelf of the coffee table, the mysterious sticky crumbs in the corners of the kitchen cupboards and the musty smell of river, cigarettes and stale beer.

One day he brought his new girlfriend to live with them on the boat. She was a Russian girl who had just moved to London. The two women would take turns keeping him company during his drinking sessions, or sometimes they both stayed with him. With the girlfriend he would behave like a little boy with his mother, lying on her lap when he got drunk, his head on her breast. With her, he would write and write.

For her birthday he got her a gerbil in a cage. It was a funny present but she felt a bit annoyed. What did she want with a gerbil? The creature didn't even like her. It tried to bite her when she took it out of its cage and was happiest when she left it alone to run in its wheel. She didn't have that much money but she had to buy it food and wood shavings to dig around in and little toys. It did look cute and sweet when it sat on its soft haunches in the wheel and didn't know she was looking. She enjoyed seeing it when she got home, curled up in the wood shavings sleeping, although she wished she could afford a dog instead.

He loved the gerbil. Now, after the drinking sessions, instead of lying on the girlfriend's lap or writing to her, he would take the gerbil out of its cage and dance around the room with it, kissing it and fondling it. He sat on the red velvet sofa for hours, caressing and cuddling the gerbil, or let it run around the room while he danced his little funny jigs to his music. He stroked its short, smooth fur so tenderly. He would rub the gerbil's fur against his cheek, feeling its tiny heart beat fast against his skin. Sometimes he would hold its small warm body in his hand, its head poking out of his fist, and lightly rub its nose with one finger. It never tried to bite him, and seemed to like him more than it liked her or anyone else.

Now after he had been out he would rush back to the boat to see the gerbil and take it out of its cage to play with. He even played with it during the daytime, before he had his first drink. She would meet the girlfriend's eyes and they both felt a mixture of fondness and sadness as they watched him with the gerbil. He had mostly stopped writing to her, but he still did it once in a while, when he had a real session.

One night she was trying unsuccessfully to go to sleep. She had been looking out of the portholes and at the moon for hours, and at the silver egg that hung from a red velvet ribbon above her bed. She could see her reflection in the egg, and the captain's room. Finally she decided to go upstairs. He was there on the velvet sofa, with a bottle of red wine on the table and the gerbil in his hands, petting it. She sat down beside him and poured herself a glass of wine. He let the gerbil run around the room as he wrote to her, the usual things. About how he loved the gerbil, and some wild stories about how his friend had had a Picasso painting secretly taken out from Kuwait and he was helping to sell it, and could she help him? She laughed and nodded and looked out at the water and at him, at the bags under his eyes and his crazy grin.

Suddenly they both looked around. Where was the gerbil? He jumped up and dashed around the room, searching for it, and she got up too and looked under the chairs and the tables. Suddenly, he turned quickly and raggedly from the wall to the heavy gold and red velvet sofa, throwing it over on its back with a huge crash to look underneath it, and she felt startled and scared. The next thing she knew he was crying with his mouth open, the flesh moist and glistening. She went over to where he was kneeling behind the sofa, his back round and vulnerable. The gerbil was wriggling flat on the floor, its back legs writhing in a different direction to its front legs, its chest dented.

She turned away, not wanting to see the tiny warm creature in such pain, not wanting to see him, either. She brought a finger across her neck.

'You have to kill it,' she said.

She felt the floor shake once and then he was going outside to the water to dump the gerbil's body into the river.

Afterwards he couldn't stop crying. He sat in the corner of the sofa, his head in his hands and his shoulders shaking.

'Do you blame me?' he wrote again and again. 'I'm so sorry.' She didn't blame him, not at all, and she told him so. But she didn't know what else she could say to him now or what she could do for him. So she just stayed there, next to him on the red velvet sofa in front of the river, as he cried and drank and wrote to her for hours.

Everything flooded into her. She felt she couldn't stand it any more, being there on the boat with pages of his wine-stained words lying around, taking up so much space and smelling up the boat, but adding nothing of relief for either of them. His words looked pathetically dead on the page. She didn't know what she could do about that.

BLACK AND
WHITE DOG

All she remembered of the first house they'd lived in was a short scene in a yellow kitchen with sunlight streaming in through the window. Her father had just come home from running. She thought she remembered that he had been wearing his Hang Loose Maui pale blue T-shirt, with shorts, but maybe that was another memory that had got mixed up with the yellow one. But she was sure that he had been making waffles, and that she had been perched on the kitchen counter next to the yellow mixing bowl her mother still had, watching her father beat together all the ingredients.

They had moved out of that house when she was two – so maybe the memory hadn't been so accurate anyway – and into the one they'd lived in ever since. They had bought the new house from a music teacher and her husband. The neighbours on the right had been very annoyed by her students' incessant banging on the piano, and when they found out that a deaf family had bought the house and were moving in they were so happy that a steady stream of cookies and cakes came from them for a while. They were the kind of heavy sweet things that coated your mouth with sugar, the kind her mother disapproved of: M&M cookies, treats with rainbow chips, white Betty Crocker cakes with store-bought frosting layered on thickly.

Later, when the neighbours realized that deaf people weren't exactly the quietest people in the world either, the cakes and cookies stopped coming.

When they first moved in, the bedroom that would be hers and her sister's was painted bright blue, almost neon. The floors had thick matted carpets, some with stains left by the previous owners. Her father had torn them all up, repainted the rooms, broken down some walls. She loved tagging along after him and going to the hardware store with him: boxes and boxes of nails all the same size, screwdrivers in descending order, black brackets on one rack and white brackets on another.

When he had thrown out all the carpets and sanded and varnished the wooden floors underneath, they would bang on the floor in one room and whoever was in the next room would feel the vibrations. It was reassuring, because sometimes you would be in a room by yourself and have no idea if anyone else was home and where they might be. Of course, sometimes Beth wished for that – not knowing where the rest of the family was and just being by herself.

But most of the time they all would be banging around, the wood floors shaking and jumping. Their black and white dog barked all the time too. The family joke was that the dog could smell hearing people, because whenever a hearing person came to the house – a door-to-door salesman, or a Jehovah's Witness in a painfully neat suit, or one of the few people they knew in the neighbourhood – the dog would get caught up in an almost ecstatic frenzy of barking, her body jerking and twisting. When deaf people came to the house the dog would only bark a few times and then settle down to her usual graceful trot round the house.

For a long time Beth believed that the dog actually could smell hearing people, that they had a strange scent all their own. It made sense when she thought about it. Deaf people communicated with their bodies. Their language was physical. She thought deaf people actually did look different from hearing people, because they looked at people more directly, not like hearing people with their shifting eyes that seemed uncomfortable when they met yours. Also, deaf people had a different quality to their bodies. They stood differently, more heavily – or maybe it was more firmly. Most hearing people felt flighty and nervous to her. So why shouldn't they smell different? She thought they probably smelled a bit acid, although she'd never got close enough to a hearing person to really smell them.

Later she realized that it was just the unfamiliar sound of hearing people's voices that the dog was reacting to. The dog was used to the guttural deaf voices they all had, except for her sister, who could hear a bit more than the rest of them and spoke more like a hearing person.

Her father would sometimes tell Beth and her sister and brother to go with him to the big bathroom, the one with the tub, and then he would shout in the tiled corner as they clustered around him, feeling his body vibrate and shake. The corner shook sharply with his voice and they would all giggle. That was when the neighbour who used to give them cookies would come to the house and ring the flashing-light doorbell, standing on the porch with disapproval clenching at her so that her face looked drawn and tight, and a paper and a pen in her hand. 'I know you all don't realize it, but you all are making a lot of noise and we can hear it next door. Could you please try to be more aware of yourself?' That was the sort of thing the paper would say.

Beth sometimes went over to her best friends' house. Joy and Mary were twins, skinny where she was square and solid. The rest of their big family were hearing except for one brother, Chris. They were allowed to roam around their neighbourhood however they wanted, and to eat from their fridge whenever they liked. In the kitchen were potato chips, store-brand

Coke in big plastic bottles, and candy. Lots of broken toys were all around the house. Sometimes she was unsure how to behave with their hearing family, but mostly she just left them alone and they left her alone and it was somewhat of a relief. She loved her own family but it felt as if there wasn't enough room between them. They all seemed more insistent and certain than she felt.

She liked to sleep over at the twins' house, but when they all stayed awake gossiping about the boys in school she would laugh too loudly and try to muffle her voice with a pillow. It never worked, and the twins' father would come angrily and sleepily to their room in his maroon-and-navy-striped robe and shout at them. Once he told them that the neighbours across the road had heard her laughing in the middle of the night and thought a wild beast was rampaging in the road.

Her parents had a party for the people who worked at the deaf school. The guests milled around the house but the centre of the party was the living room, the room with the white sofas that they used only rarely, and mostly for special dinners or posing for family photos or parties. Beth stayed by the table with the food, nibbling and watching people talk to one another. There was a man, a close friend of her parents, whom she had never really taken to. He had curly brown hair – a bit thin now, she noticed – and an affable manner that never felt to her as if it reached warmth. She secretly watched him talk to some other people. Neither of her parents was in the room – her mother was in the kitchen, and her father was somewhere else, probably shooting a few hoops in the yard with his friends.

She saw the man look around and say to someone else: 'You see the yard? So messy, they could do a lot more with it. The house ain't too bad, but . . . They're strange. But that's them, you know, that's how they are. Of course they're friends, but. You know what I'm saying?'

She felt shocked and disturbed, almost humiliated. She wondered if he knew that she was in the room, and looked down at the food, not wanting him to see that she had seen what he had said, right there in their living room. It felt blasphemous to her. She wondered if she should tell her parents about their friend's betrayal, but she also wanted to forget right away what she had just seen and for them not to know, and also she didn't want to be reminded of it by anything that her parents might do, by any lasting resentment of their friend she would sense in them.

In the end she decided not to say anything about it to anyone, but the moment stayed with her. It was as if some very thin membrane she had always thought was around them and their house had been punctured, carelessly, just for the hell of it, out of pure, narrow stupidity.

Now freezing cold air swept right in through the hole and chilled her to the bone. When she thought about her house and her family, she didn't feel protected any more.

The first time her eyes met Tommy's was at a basketball game, across the bleachers. She had heard stories about him before that, and seen some pictures. He had lazy green eyes. His teeth were very white, and even in the pictures he had a kind of lopsided grace. He looked like he was always ready to leave wherever he was easily and without fuss, and he made everyone else around him seem as if they were stuck where they were. There were other things there in him, but she didn't want or need to see anything else.

The first time they kissed was on a church rooftop near his mother's house. Tommy could climb anywhere, and he pulled her up after him, making her feel as light as he was. They sat there, teetering on the very point of the steep high roof, with a bottle of Southern Comfort between them. The cars went by on the dark main road next to the church, with their white headlights and red tail lights. Everyone else was far down below in the parking lot. There was even a catfight going on, with Marie the big-breasted blonde getting violently drunk on purpose to get attention from the guy she fancied. She was crying and screaming, but of course she made sure that her shoulders were thrown back so that her breasts were high and ready for battle.

But on the roof with Tommy, she was so far away from all of it. He had brought up a pad of lined white paper for them to talk on, with a thick black pen and a flashlight to read the words by. It was strange that they couldn't even talk properly, but they didn't care that much about it. He said he would learn sign language. He seemed instinctively to understand how to be around deaf people, not like most hearing people. He never asked her stupid questions, but at the same time, when they were with hearing people and it got to her and she felt lonely and clumsy and stupid, not know-ing where to put her eyes and her body, he knew it and would find a gentle way to be with her.

The liquor store let them have booze even though they were under age. It was run by Mexicans. When Beth went in to buy her Southern Comfort the Mexicans would always wave to her and hold up a thumb to see if she was good. She'd say, Yeah, thumbs up, or sometimes thumbs down, Not so good, or wave her hand back and forth, So-so, and ask how they were. They joked with her, saluting sharply when she had her sailor jacket on, or telling her not to drink the alcohol she was buying all by herself. She'd mime hold-ing three bottles to her mouth at the same time and downing them all, and then stagger around. They'd laugh with big open mouths and shake a finger at her.

She read on their lips, No, no, no, little girl! No, no, no!

When Tommy went into the liquor store with her for the first time Beth wondered if he would stand back when the Mexicans gestured to her, as so many hearing people did, with their fake smiles of discomfort. But Tommy laughed when the Mexicans told her not to drink too much. With two fingers he drew a line from his eyes to her: Don't you worry. I'm watching her.

She loved the lines at the sides of his mouth when he smiled. She knew they would stay there through whatever happened. She could imagine him as an old man with those same lines on a different face. They came often, too. He smiled easily, not like the people in her family. And from the first time she had seen him, that smile felt familiar to her, as if she had felt it before somehow. She knew that her own smile was very different, but on the inside it felt like his.

When she and Tommy wanted to get away from their lives, but had no money to go anywhere, they would pitch a tent by the side of the highway, far enough away from the road and under enough trees that they felt concealed. Finally alone, they would be together all night, away from everything else. Other times they had enough money and they would drive down the coast of Baja California in his small brown pickup truck with his surfboard in the back. He drove,

Beth sat by him, and sometimes she laid her head in his lap and looked up at him, at his nose and mouth and his muscles moving as he shifted gear.

Beth knew she had to bring him home at some point, to meet her family, but she wasn't sure when would be the right time. Finally she thought, what the hell, and invited him over.

He walked into the house, her beloved, beautiful Tommy, and the black and white dog ran up to him and barked, her body twisting uncontrollably in the air.

Her mother laughed and wrote to Tommy on a piece of white paper, 'The dog can smell hearing people.'

Tommy was more familiar to her than almost any-thing. They had been together so easily, and now she knew that every time he brought her home the black and white dog would bark like that again and her mother would say the same thing, and the same violent puncture that her parents' friend had made in her idea of her family would be made again in what she felt about Tommy.

She knew suddenly that if she had told her parents what their friend had said, they wouldn't have cared at all, not really. She still cared, still disliked that man intensely, all those years later.

She didn't know how she could protect herself now, and protect Tommy, too. She hated the idea of risking that tenderness in herself and in him. She felt for the agile muscles in his upper arm that she knew so well and led him to see the back yard, away from her mother and the dog.

THE VELVET ROPE

The girls sipped their drinks in front of the mirror as they put on their make-up. Dana had bought new bronze eyeshadow for them to wear, but it was sticky and gathered in the creases above Jade's eyes. Melly wore her usual expensive make-up in neutral colours. They crowded the mirror, blow-drying their hair and wondering who might be at the club they were going to. On the way to the beach the week before, stuck in a traffic jam on the freeway, the girls whiled away the time their favourite way. They made up stories about the people in the other cars.

The puffy woman in the beat-up Honda with the grey patches on the outside of the car and the McDonald's wrappers in the back seat? She had a faded pink smiley-face air freshener tangled up with the Mardi Gras beads that dangled from her rear-view mirror. She would be called Yolanda, and she would live with her boyfriend in a small apartment in the Valley with the TV on all the time and a dirty refrigerator. They would have sex on the sofa during the commercials, him occasionally gripping the sides of her pleasantly chunky tummy, leaving red marks. He really did love her, but her girlfriends would always tell her she deserved better.

Then there was the man muttering non-stop into his mobile, hanging on to the steering wheel of his red convertible for dear life. The girls couldn't see his eyes under his dark sunglasses, and they couldn't tell what he was talking about so seriously. They guessed it was probably some big business deal or some exclusive restaurant he was trying to get a reservation at, maybe in Beverly Hills. They fantasized about what they would wear if he were taking them out to dinner. Jade said she would wear a short bright pink dress with puffed sleeves and matching peep-toe heels, but Dana said that was much too obvious. Dana thought that any girl who went out with a man like that should wear something black, calf-length, but with a V-neck and just a bit of cleavage peeping out. Melly said she would wear a long flowing dress, with her hair down, and high-heeled sandals with ribbons that she could wrap around her legs and tie in a floppy bow. They pulled up alongside the man's car and waved to him. He jerked his head around, startled and annoyed, and then his head went back to look forward again, straight at the road, as he went on muttering on his phone.

Men like that one last week might be at the club tonight, but a bit more relaxed, of course.

They downed the last of their drinks and set off for

the car. The club wasn't far away from the apartment and they rolled down the windows. It was getting dark, and the air felt warm and familiar on their clean skin. The road was crowded with cars filled with hard bright people heading out and soft tired people heading home from work. The car in front had a fuzzy toy dog on the back window ledge. Its head shook steadily as the car wormed forward. It had painted black eyes, with the paint chipped off one eye, so that it looked to be winking or one-eyed.

Dana pulled forward with the aggressive driving style she'd learned from a boyfriend who went off-roading in his 4×4.

They passed the car with the nodding dog and saw the two people in the front seats. The driver was a skinny man with a flat boxer's nose and a Virgin Mary painted on his white T-shirt. Small pink pimples clustered in the centres of his cheeks beneath his yellow Oakley sunglasses. A blonde girl in a tight sky blue tank top sat next to him, the red silk strap of her bra sitting outside her shirt. Jesus on the cross hung from the black plastic rosary beads suspended on the rear-view mirror, swaying almost in time with the one-eyed dog in the back. The man had his arm draped over the steering wheel and his seat pushed way back.

His head moved rhythmically, forward and then back. It seemed musical because he was moving his shoulders in time, too, and he was mouthing words that the girls could catch the outlines of. They were music words like 'Oh baby'. The girl in the seat next to him was snapping her fingers and mouthing the same words, so obviously a song was playing on the radio. Suddenly the regularity broke as the man turned to the girl, shouting at her in erratic bursts that had a different look to them. The big round muscles of his arm tensed and loosened with his shouts. He looked like a rooster. The blonde girl looked out the window, not paying attention to him. The girls wondered what he was saying.

But soon the blonde girl slid over to kiss him, so it must be all right.

They pulled up to the club and the black velvet rope. A squat Mexican valet in white shirt and black pants rushed up to take their keys. The club would have looked like any other unmarked store in the beige concrete building if there hadn't been a line of girls in high heels and men in jeans around the corner. There were paparazzi by the entrance, too, soft-bellied men in T-shirts, looking with sharp eyes at who went in and out in case there was someone famous. Jade was the one who knew the bouncer from when they'd worked together, so she pushed forward through the crowd up by the rope. The bouncer didn't look especially thrilled to see her, but he nodded and waved them through. Soon they were inside the club, and everyone else in the line looked at them walking in, asses swinging and calf muscles working hard above the stiletto heels.

Inside, they decided to check the place out before getting a drink. Jade and Dana knew people. Melly only went out with them occasionally, so she lagged behind, a bit uncertain. Her dress suddenly felt too short and too tight over her ass and she tugged at its hem. Jade was pointing out people to them. There was a football player, huge diamonds in his ears, leaning against the bar. And there was a rapper-turned-actor Jade had once flirted with at the end of a long night at another club, and she had told everyone about him. Tonight when she waved at him his eyes slid coolly over the three of them with no sign of recognition. He was watching the door.

A guy none of them had met before came up to them and started whispering in Jade's ear. He was cute, but they had met pretty boys like him before: hair cut to look just a bit shaggy and overgrown, plaid shirt that was supposed to look grungy but was clearly designer by the looks of its sewn-on patches. Jade wagged a finger at him and pointed at her ears.

'Me no hear . . .'

Then she gestured a cup moving to her lips.

'Drink?'

Three Red Bulls and vodka were soon on the bar, but the guy had spotted someone else he wanted to talk to. Dana and Melly low-fived Jade anyway. A free drink – good job, honey. The Red Bulls and vodka were rose pink and translucent and a wet mist lay on the glasses.

Melly went to stand in line for the ladies' room,

where she could shut herself in a cubicle for some time without being noticed. The cold metal walls of the toilet stall were reassuring. She was alone except for the stiletto heels she could see in the next stall. Two sets of heels, she noticed, one pair scarlet red with matching laces up the tan legs and the other silver-sequinned, leading up to plump orange-freckled legs. Probably doing coke in there, although she preferred to think of them talking: maybe a crisis with a boyfriend. Outside the stall in the club she knew everyone was looking at everyone else, deciding what they thought and what they wanted.

When she went back outside to find Jade and Dana, the club was now full of people. They stood in twos and threes on the square dance floor, some swaying their hips. The rapper-turned-actor had found who he was looking for, a blonde model Melly recognized from a magazine ad. He was dancing close to her, his lips moving softly against the side of her head. Melly leaned against the bar and watched them murmur to one another. She wondered at the thoughts that left them so confidently. By that time she had a fragile sense of what most of their exchanges would be like. She didn't feel like she could hold on to any of the conversations she had had in places like this.

She looked around and found Jade and Dana with a huge man who she remembered from another party. His name was Chunky and he always had coke and he always knew where an after-party was. Jade could hear more than the others and she could speak pretty well, so she was talking with Chunky. Sometimes she translated for Dana and Melly, but not always. Not this time.

Dana had written to his friend on a pad in her deaf English.

'I am move here with friend mine. I had wonderful time this here since. I was work in bar. I will look other job now. You are interesting to show me more around this city? You know where party?'

Chunky was talking to his friends about Dana, Melly thought, but she couldn't understand what he was saying. She only saw his eyes and one of his hands on Dana's arse.

They left to go on to a party Chunky knew about.

Outside the club Melly saw a bum sitting against the wall just beyond the velvet rope as they were walking by, his hands around his bent knees. His eyes met hers for much longer than anyone inside the club had looked at her. Under his red knitted cap his eyes were watery and very bright blue in his creased face. When the bum looked down at her high heels she saw the words 'Beautiful shoes' on his lips. She was wearing her tweed Prada heels that her boss had given her, and they really were beautiful. She saw that Chunky's yellow Hummer was at the kerb, waiting for them to follow him in Dana's car. She had to go. She reached into her purse and found all the money that she had, and gave it to the bum. It was less than the cost of the Red Bull and vodka that the guy in the club had bought for her. The bum clutched at her leg, and she wanted to stay and talk with him, but she had to shake free and go.

They had to walk down many flights of lit-up marble steps to get to the sunken entryway of the apartment building where the party was. They were all excited because it was in a fancy part of Beverly Hills where they'd never been before. Who knew who they'd meet?

The large room had the same marble floor as the stairs outside, but the marble that had looked sensual outside felt cold inside. Three plasma screens were lined up along the wall to the left of the door. Porn was playing on all of them. The few things that were in the room were all white, black, or silver, except for the people. Four men, no women. They didn't have much colour to them either. There was an oblong silver bowl right in the middle of the square glass and steel coffee table. It was filled to the brim with white grains. The men's bodies spilled over onto the black leather sofas. They didn't exactly look alike – one had slicked-back silver hair and red cheeks, another a brown comb-over and a pink shirt – but they felt alike. They were a specific kind of overweight, not beer-bellied and spreading like the paparazzi photographers and not red-meat-and-drip-pings stocky like the valets. These men were doughy from long nights and long days of booze and rich food in expensive restaurants. If you put a nose in the folds of their necks they would smell of Italian musk cologne, but under that they would smell sour.

Their eyes looked from the girls to the silver bowl to the television screens with equal interest.

Chunky led them to the kitchen, where row upon row of liquor bottles were lined up. They started drinking and Chunky started talking, about his mother, and his babysitter when he was a little boy, and how he had come to California, and how those fucking people always ripped him off all the time. Jade translated for Dana and Melly. It went on.

Melly and Dana clutched hands. They knew they both felt there and not there, remembering what Chunky was saying yet not remembering, or maybe they had forgotten, or never had known. Did they know what he was saying? It all was mixed up and dissolved.

They broke free and wandered around the rooms. In the bathroom another man floated naked in the bathtub, eyes tightly shut. Asleep or high or both. He was holding on to his fleshy pink willy and his legs were akimbo at the sides of the tub.

It was funny. Melly and Dana had made up stories about the people in the cars on the highway, but there was little temptation to make up stories about any of the men in the apartment. Melly and Dana knew there was susceptibility in these men, but this night seemed to leach it out of them. Dana had tried to talk to the man in the pink shirt, but she said he felt like Chunky, the words acting only as a release.

They suddenly remembered Jade, alone in the kitchen with Chunky, and went to find her. They needed to go home. A naked woman with perfectly round breasts walked out of one of the rooms whose doors had been shut and they saw an unmade white bed behind her. She had been in there all along. More silent women.

They came back to Jade, who was still trying to understand Chunky. She was peering at his mouth, nodding, interested.

—Finish, he stupid talk, Dana signed to Melly.

—Me feel bad for him but me really mood go home now. Me not like stay with him for what? This weird place. Me ban us with him again for future.

Melly wanted to go home too. Jade was drunk and coked up but she wasn't under Chunky's spell. She found a pen in one of the drawers, some free Bic pen from an insurance company, and ripped off the label from one of the vodka bottles.

'Thanks for taking us here, but I gotta work tomorrow and I think we better go,' she wrote on the back of the vodka label.

It took time to get Chunky to shut up for long enough to read the note, and when he did he shook one of his thick fingers at her.

'No, you stay here girls. We ain't finished yet.'

66

—Finish, Dana signed again. Me really not want stay here. Fuck.

They leaned against the kitchen counter and allowed themselves to be hypnotized by the gaping maw of his mouth, lips slapping and sashaying in a ridiculous dance, his eyes burning with emotion that didn't transmit to them. He knew that they didn't understand, but he wanted to talk anyway. There wasn't anything else for it but to wait.

Melly casually walked into the other room and tried the front door of the apartment. It was locked. The man with the brown comb-over and the pink shirt shifted on the couch, his eyes slowly leaving the porn on the TV to shake an open palm at her. So that was a no-go too. She drifted back into the kitchen to watch Chunky some more.

In the main room the entire back wall was taken up by a window. They knew it looked out on the beach, but the white vertical blinds were drawn so tight that none of the luminous light of the night showed through from outside. Inside, fluorescent bulbs glared down on them. You could see everything on everyone's faces, the broken vessel beneath Dana's left eye and the black mole above Chunky's right eyebrow. The tiny details of their faces seemed as if they would be familiar for life, although rationally once they got out of this place the details would fade fast. The crash was coming soon.

When it came, the balance of the night would shift

fast. The bubble would burst and the detached curiosity that had characterized the evening would cease to be enough protection for them. Maybe they would finally be allowed to leave then, at least.

—We go now, Dana said. Please.

She grabbed hold of Chunky and shook him. With the fingers of one hand she beckoned to him.

—Keys now. We have to go. You shush. No more blab blab, blab, talk, talk, talk. Stop it now. Her forefinger sliced sharply through the sluggish atmosphere of the room.

He looked startled, suddenly outside everything he'd been saying.

—He says he sorry, Jade told the other two. He said he really good person. He not mean do that. He very, very, sorry. He said he not like other fuckers in this city. We need careful but he good man.

He led the girls into the other room and demanded the key from the silver-haired man. Soon the door was open, and they could leave. As Jade, Melly, and Dana stepped outside the door, Chunky put a hand on Melly's shoulder and stopped her.

'I'm sorry,' she read on his lips. 'Take care.'

He hugged her. He smelled of new cotton T-shirts and of sweat beneath that. Melly turned to leave but he kept her inside the hug for a moment more.

She followed Jade and Dana up the shimmering steps, and they all wandered onto the beach in front of the building. There was a full moon and nobody else was on the beach. They took off their high heels and pushed their bare feet into the crumbly damp sand as they walked, stopping just before the water line to sit down. It was windy and fresh. Already the scenes inside the apartment felt securely in the past, but the evening hadn't turned into a funny party story yet. Some more time for that. For now they just sat and looked out on the water. Melly rested her head on Dana's shoulder. They were very tired.

ABEL, GRANNY
AND HIM

When she was little there was a boy at her school who had only started classes when he was thirteen or fourteen. He was called Abel. Before then he had stayed at home. In the daytime he sat in the dirt in the yard. He rocked back and forth to amuse himself. Sometimes he bit his lip until he drew blood. Every few weeks, regular as rain, he erupted and threw a fit, rolling in the yard and screaming. His mother never knew how to quiet him. She couldn't even tell him what his name was. He could tell them when he needed to piss or shit, or when he was hungry or thirsty. By the time they found out that he was deaf and not retarded and sent him to the deaf school, it was too late and he had very little language his whole life.

He sat in class with a false smile on his face, repeating what people signed to him.

—I happy, I happy, he nodded, but she wondered if he understood what happiness was.

He seemed to know that sex existed but he just knew it as an urge. He didn't even know that the idea of death existed, or the idea of God. She knew this because she had seen Abel's teacher tell her teacher a story, passed on by Abel's mother. For some years in the long period before Abel went to school, his family had a pet canary. Abel often watched the canary hopping around, flying in short bursts in its cage and pecking at its seeds. One day it had died and Abel had thrown his worst fit, not understanding where the canary had gone. Without the ideas of death, a higher power, or any afterlife to console him, he was distraught.

She thought of Abel often, and especially when her granny came to visit just before she died. Her granny's body had become small and fragile without anybody really noticing. She laughed all the time, and when they went on the public bus she pulled Jolene's top down and giggled at her exposed bra. When they walked by the river, her granny thought it was the river near where she had grown up, even though they were on the other side of the world. When she looked up and saw a handsome young man, she flirted spicily.

She didn't know death or time existed either, Jolene was sure of it, not during that part of her life. Once Jolene had flagged down a taxi and her granny had said, 'Everyone in this city loves you! I can't believe it! People stop in the streets to give you rides in their cars!' The way her granny responded was completely different to the things that set her off.

Her granny made her think of Abel. Both of them

seemed to be outside everything, but actually they were outside language and ideas. Sometimes in certain solitary moments she thought she could reach this place, like a pool you could dive into and stay submerged in, letting the water play over your body for ever.

She remembered a few times when it had felt as if she had caught a glimpse of the place, sometimes during sex or when she was fucked up. But it was rare, and after those few perfectly cloistered moments were over it was gone again. It was like trying to jump over your own shadow, or escape from it. Could you? She thought so.

When she thought about Abel and her granny it brought back that feeling of being far outside the usual ways of seeing and thinking.

In her teens, she'd had an annoying habit of always asking people to explain their ideas to her, or to explain what other people were like, or what she seemed like, or how she looked. But their answers always left something out. When she tried to tell other people what she thought they were like, she knew she left a lot of things out, too.

She remembered the time she'd had a lover who asked her out to dinner on some pretext so flimsy it was almost funny, but it was also exciting. Their real motives were known to them both, for sure. Sitting across from him at the table, the feeling was strong and true in her gut, and it was strong in him, she knew, even though they were talking about the weather.

The huge gap between what was being said and what was happening underneath excited and scared her. But she had thought he would stop, and when they stepped out into the parking lot onto the asphalt that was sticky and smelling of tar in the summer heat, he turned to her and kissed her, smooth, delicate, his fingers light in her hair. She felt herself in that pool, and it was bottomless. Then suddenly he stopped and walked beside her to the car, talking about the weather again.

They spent months moving between the weather and the bottomless pool. It made her confused and dizzy. She could think of nothing but him, his skin, the shape of his fingers, the freckles he had on his eyelids. They slept together every night but it wasn't enough. Once at a party she was outside on the balcony when he came upstairs, and in the middle of a crowd of people, as he talked to her, just looking at him took her away.

She was sure he was in the pool, too, but he wouldn't talk about it. She cried a lot from the feeling of disorientation. She had no idea where she was. She felt like he could have told her where she was, where they were, but he refused. Or maybe she was doing the same thing she had done when she was younger, asking people to tell her what things were when they couldn't.

One day they were walking by the river. They had been with a group of friends but they had somehow become separated and found themselves alone. It didn't matter to her where they were going, just so long as he was next to her. Yet she was thin-skinned from the anxiety. At first the gap between what they were doing and what lay beneath it had been exhilarating, but it was too much for her to sustain over a long period. Maybe if there had been certainty in him it wouldn't have been a big deal. If they had more time on their own it would have been okay. But they were often with a big crowd of people and he was always rocking or shaking in some way. He was continually shifting balance between one foot and the other or breaking off in the middle of talking with one person to talk to the entire group, entertaining them with an anecdote and then moving quickly on to the next story. Even then by the river, he was telling her a story about something vaguely funny one of his friends had said. She nodded and laughed, but her mind and the whole of her self weren't there.

After that long, chaotic period she had gone away. He hadn't tried to contact her. When she saw him again after nearly a year, he acted as if she'd never been away. As if everything was the same, coming up to talk to her about some stupid thing and looking at her in the same transporting way as before.

It would have been easy if everything *was* the same. But down in the bottom of herself, something blistered made her go away from him.

That wasn't the end of it, not by half, but it had been

something definitive to do. She had to do something, wasn't that right? She didn't really know.

Very little of what people said to her when she told them about him (she had to talk about him, it was the only thing she could think about and she couldn't conceal it) felt as if it had much relation to the reality of him standing in front of her, the feeling that lay hopelessly there between them. In some ways she felt as if she was turning into a strange version of him, chattering away about things that no reply could soothe. But she couldn't stay quiet either.

By that time she had almost forgotten about Abel. He was a small part of her childhood in a place that felt far from where she was now. From time to time he popped into her mind, but somehow she never connected him to the rest her life. She didn't even know where he was. She imagined him drifting from job to job. Possibly drinking a lot. Finding women who probably manipulated and provoked him. She hoped she was wrong, though, and he had found someone nice. Unlike her.

She found herself thinking more about Abel around the time she'd told her lover to go. Perhaps it was because she felt more like him than she had ever felt before: with no real idea of what was going on around her, and prone to outbursts. Then she thought about her granny. Towards the end of her life, she'd had absolutely no idea of what was going on around her, either, but she

had just gone her way, and found her way to that bottomless pool without anyone bringing her there.

It was a long time before she could think about that
lover. But finally she did it, and she was okay then.

KING EDDIE

Laura had taught herself to pee standing up because she was so fascinated with King Eddie. She wondered what it felt like to be him.

She had seen him around, at basketball tournaments and football games. And everyone talked about him – not always directly, but he lurked at the centre of stories. Many people worked for him, and many others had gone to parties at his big house up in the hills. He was a threatening presence in some of the stories, fatherly and protective in others. Laura knew Eddie went to the deaf club every Wednesday night, the night when everyone came after work to socialize. Sometimes she had driven with her mother to drop her father off at the club, and had gone inside briefly so her mother could show her off to everyone. Eddie was always there, full of qualities she didn't entirely understand, but she had never stayed there long enough to get a firmer grip on her idea of him.

Laura didn't dare tell her mother about the peeing, though. Neither her parents nor their friends exactly approved of Eddie. She would sneak into the kitchen when her parents' friends were there and stay against a wall, watching what they said about the people they all knew. They talked often about him. But there were stories about him that they would stop telling when she was in the room. No matter how quiet she was, trying to make them forget she was there.

When they were growing up, her mother and King Eddie had gone to the same school and they both had deaf families. Her mother signed beautifully. When you watched her telling stories you were intoxicated by the certainty of her movements. Laura loved asking for stories about people they knew, just so she could watch. Her mother knew about everybody's families, too.

Her mother would say, when Laura asked about King Eddie:

—You know who my friend Mike, we grow up together? Big man, sweet, curly hair, little bit cross-eye? Wife fat? Anyway, really Mike self-brother Eddie, but they different, wow. Really parents, them-two good people, deaf both, never college, Eddie father-self work hard printer same your grandpa. Union together. Mike, good man, same father. Eddie, bad boy, party-party always.

Her mother would flare a nostril, crook an eyebrow, and chew on a piece of imaginary gum at that point in the story, becoming Eddie as a salty young tough.

Then she carried on:

—Later Eddie older, meet Amy, she-self grow up hearing world, shy, never met deaf, she overwhelm meet Eddie, Eddie flirt-flirt, charm her, grab her finish. That, marry, them-two since together. But she not tend out-out, most stay home with kids. Eddie alone go all gatherings, nightlife.

It was summer, no school. Laura was going up into junior high, so her mother had said she could go to the deaf club tonight with them. All the regulars would be there, Eddie certainly. She was excited to see what they all got up to, especially Eddie. Her younger brother had to stay with the family around the corner. He was too young to go to the club, her mother said.

They had a quick dinner because they were going out. It was Laura's favourite, home-made macaroni and cheese with a crusty top. They ate it with cooked frozen peas mixed in. After the washing up was done and her brother had been walked around the corner with his dark green sleeping bag and a toothbrush, flannel pyjamas and a change of Hanes' tighty-whitie briefs in his Mickey Mouse backpack, Laura set off for the deaf club with her parents in their station wagon. It wasn't far, but it was on the other side of town and she watched the tract houses of their neighbourhood change into the bright streetlights and the McDonald's joints, Taco Bells and Jack in the Boxes of Main Street, and then they were into the square apartment blocks and occasional boarded–up Victorian houses of the area around the deaf club.

As they pulled into the parking lot, Laura saw King Eddie's fire engine red vintage convertible in his spot right by the front door. It stood out from all the other cars, mostly sedans, with the occasional station wagon or pickup truck thrown in.

The lobby was crowded with people ordering beer from the bar at the end of the room furthest from the front door. Laura stayed close to her parents as they said hello to everyone and worked their way slowly into the main room. She smiled at whoever her parents were talking to and thanked people when they remarked on how big she had gotten. As soon as they entered the main room, she saw King Eddie in his chair in the corner.

As usual, Ricky was next to Eddie's chair, moving anxiously from foot to foot. Ricky had one eye a little higher than the other and a flat, broken nose. There was a patch of blotched pigment on his face like the freckles on the pale pink of a dog's belly. Luckily he seemed not to know how he looked. It suited King Eddie to have someone like Ricky around.

Ricky worked on the streets with the rest of King Eddie's army, selling cards with the sign-language alphabet on them. Most of the others were like Ricky, people who weren't sure of their reading and writing abilities. Most of them had hearing families they couldn't communicate with. There weren't many jobs in the deaf community, and if you worked for someone hearing it was lonely. They preferred to work for King Eddie. He talked to them, he soothed them and he made them feel protected and supported. And the job was easy.

They worked on the streets or in trains, walking dutifully up one side of the train and down the other, passing out cards with the sign-language finger-spelled alphabet on one side and the words 'I'm deaf, I can't work, I need money, please give me some' on the other. Then they walked back around to collect, either taking the cards back or picking up money. The money went to Eddie later.

Occasionally they bumped into another deaf person, someone more educated and in gainful employment, who said things like:

—You make deaf community look bad, you stop, get real job!

But they were under Eddie's protection. He was an imposing man, with a high, greasy Elvis-style pompadour on top becoming a curly mullet that spilled onto his shoulders, and heavy gold chains around his neck and both wrists. People said he had a big house up in the hills with stone lions at the top of a long brick driveway and a jacuzzi in the living room.

Tonight he was telling one of his stories and there was a crowd round him. Not many of Laura's parents' friends were there, but she could see Jamie, whose son

Mario was in Laura's class at school. Jamie's pale blue eyes were intent on Eddie as she bent forward to be a little closer to the King and his story.

Laura loved it when Jamie came to school to pick up Mario. Her perfume smelled like flowery baby powder and her smile came often and warm. She had slender arms and wore bright colours, mostly pink and purple, with beaded dangly earrings. She worked in the post office, where everyone else on her shift was hearing, and her parents had never learned to sign.

Eddie started his story.

—Me work, work, many-years, you all know.

He was large even in his gestures. A fluid extravagance found its way into everything he did.

—Me build-build business, bring people in, work together. Cooperate. Support each other. Work for future.

He stretched out his hand into the space in front of him, reaching as far as he could as he signed the word 'future'.

—Must think future. Must plan strategy for future. Not think now all time. Plus, we deaf, even more must work together. I go Mexico for what, vacation, I with wife mine, walk beach. It different world. Junk throw-around streets everywhere, donkey with cart trot past, people all poor small broken-roof houses. Not like here America. All Mexicans look up-down me and wife, why, we white. We enter restaurant, eat, all people look up-down us. Me see what? Two Mexican man sit corner, they see me and wife us-two sign, they come-up us. Find they deaf same. They invite us his home. They treat us like family. Cook big dinner, feast, drink all night, all tell funny story many, all laugh. Easy communicate, easy understand simple gestures. He job not have, struggle feed family, sell rings, bracelets, necklaces, street. Deaf world all over, same. Deaf same. Hearing not understand. Us must communication, must support each other. Must. No communication how?

Everyone nodded deep in agreement. It was true, for sure.

Laura was sitting with her parents at a table by the door to the lobby and bar with her apple juice in a styrofoam cup. She bit into the side of the cup and crumbs of it fell into the juice. The foam smelled and tasted faintly chemical. She stared at Eddie and wondered what his hair cream would smell like, if she ever got close enough to him to find out.

Outside the deaf club it was dark for as far as she could see. The streetlights filtered down, with dust motes dancing slowly in their yellow light. Nobody was on the streets except for a few deaf people talking under the lights in the parking lot. The darkness didn't feel soft to Laura, as it usually did. It felt like there was a thin film of grime over everything.

Inside the club Mindy was perching on the arm of Eddie's chair, telling him how much she agreed with what he had been telling them all earlier. The fat on the bottoms of her arms shuddered when she signed to Eddie. Eddie took up the entire chair, his legs spread as wide as possible, and Mindy's fleshy bum spilled over both sides of the vinyl-coated arm.

Ricky was sitting on the floor by now, his back against the wall. He got up to go over to Eddie and Mindy, slinging his arm over Mindy's shoulder.

—Me agree with you one hundred fifty per cent! Me believe same you, for sure, Ricky signed emphatically to Mindy.

King Eddie looked lazily around at Ricky.

—Me enjoy now. Eddie's broad lips protruded to punctuate the 'enjoy'. Relax. Calm. Calm. Not have to bother-bother me all time.

Ricky looked scared.

—Sorry, Laura saw him say to Eddie, looking at the floor. I'm sorry. I not mean bother you.

Laura felt as if she shouldn't be looking at what was happening. As mesmerizing as King Eddie was to her, it felt awful to see Ricky next to him at that moment.

Eddie swept his arm around the room.

—Oh, go away. Go flirt woman if you can find one. He laughed. Have many women here, can find one? Can you? Me happy give you money buy drink for woman. Or buy drink for yourself, whatever. Not matter. Go have good time. Not must with-with me all time right? Go, go.

Ricky scuttled away fast. Jamie's husband Chris was working the bar that night. He was the football coach and he often told Laura things she wasn't supposed to know, not out of any desire to corrupt, but because he had no sense of what he was and wasn't supposed to tell her.

Chris got a bottle of Bud from the old fridge behind the bar and slid it across the counter to Ricky. The moisture on the bottom of the beer left wet skid marks on the Formica counter.

Eddie waved at Chris from his throne.

—Come on. Give him a shot of tequila too. He clapped his hands. Come on, Ricky, drink up! Have fun! It's on me!

Ricky looked around him, and at Eddie lounging on his chair and Mindy looking at him with her flat eyes.

—Come on, do it! Mindy signed to Ricky. Her forefinger cut sharply through the air as she did it. Come on!

Ricky brought the neon green plastic shot glass to his mouth and downed the cheap tequila in one go. Laura saw the muscles in his throat working as he struggled to swallow it. He was gagging slightly, but he moved to one side as he did it, so that Eddie didn't see.

—Good, me surprised, first-time think you maybe real man, Eddie said. Thumbs-up, clap–clap. See–see you can one more? Come on. Me pay you.

He waved at Chris.

—One-more down there!

Laura was fascinated. She'd seen her dad have a beer or two when watching football or basketball, or at Super Bowl, and her parents had wine with dinner sometimes. She'd even seen her mother say she mustn't have another, or she'd get tipsy. But nothing like this before. She didn't like what Eddie was doing to Ricky, and she felt more than a little guilty for watching it happen. But she was still fascinated. It was more interesting than anything she'd seen on television.

—You sure? Chris said to Ricky, but Ricky nodded vehemently, Yes, yes! So Chris poured more tequila, the colour of dark urine, into the neon green plastic glass.

King Eddie clapped again and pummelled the air with one fist.

—Go, go, Ricky!

And again he brought the glass to his mouth, but this time he wasn't able to conceal the gagging from Eddie. Ricky bent from the knees, holding his stomach with one hand and his mouth with the other. Laura saw his cheeks balloon as his shoulders heaved and he struggled not to give in and vomit. Finally he straightened up and looked around at Eddie, who was laughing and clapping one leg with his hand. Mindy, who was still balancing precariously on the arm of the chair, was looking hungrily at Eddie.

—C'mon, last one for him, Eddie said to Chris, slapping some money down on the table. He kissed Mindy hard on the mouth and got up from the low chair in one smooth motion. Putting on his black leather jacket quickly, he gave everyone in the club a collective wave goodbye before crossing the two rooms quickly with long steps. Laura saw the tail lights of his convertible shine as he halted the car briefly before driving away. Through the door of the deaf club, she saw that he had the top down. His mullet swirled as he turned the car left onto the road.

Laura's parents had been busy talking with a friend, Laura hadn't even seen what about, but someone else who had seen what happened waved to them.

—Did you see that? Poor Ricky . . .

And then Laura's mother yanked her arm.

—We're leaving now. Not appropriate for children. I never should've brought you here while Eddie here. Stupid me!

Laura would have liked to stay, to see if Ricky recovered and also to have a look at everyone else she'd not even checked out because of Eddie and Ricky. But she had no choice but to follow her parents. Her mother still had her by the arm as they barrelled out of the deaf club and into their car.

She had one last glimpse of the room. Ricky was standing unsteadily at the bar, an arm clasped tightly around his beer belly, one more glass of tequila being poured for him by Chris, whose face seemed more closed than usual. Mindy was chattering away to a woman Laura had never seen before, she was saying something about how she might be able to get a job with Eddie. And Jamie was now behind the bar with Chris, talking to him as he poured the shot.

On the drive home, Laura looked out the window as her parents discussed the evening in the front seats. People were putting out their trash cans for the garbage truck to empty in the morning. Two teenage girls with slicked-back hair were laughing in the back of a red pickup truck waiting in the line at the Taco Bell drive-in. She could see her reflection in the car window and she wondered about it. The darkness still felt like a film of grime to her. Ricky's face was constant in her mind, the hesitation on it.

And King Eddie. Where had he gone after leaving the deaf club? she wondered. Where was he now?

THE WILD MAN

In the morning when Victor got up, the first thing he did was feed the animals. It was a good way to start the day, walking out of the hut and looking down at the ocean for a minute or two, before opening the airtight plastic bin just to the left of his back door where he stored the pellets for the rabbits. He mixed in anything he had left over from his supper. He didn't eat much, though, and there was rarely a lot, just some greens he set aside from the vegetables he ate nearly every day. For the cats, he had fish heads and fish scraps in another airtight plastic bin.

The animals swarmed around the blue ceramic dishes as soon as he set them down – the rabbits' dish near their hutches at the furthest end of his little clearing in the jungle, and the cats' dish on the other side of his door from the plastic bins. He watched carefully to make sure each animal got its share. All the cats usually did, but there was one small rabbit that got bullied by the biggest rabbit, a large white male with black spots. It sometimes bit the littlest one in its greedy quest for the food, and then Victor squirted it with water from a plastic bottle he kept just inside the back door of his hut.

After he fed the animals, Victor took a shower. Rainwater was collected in a metal tank mounted on stilts, just by the edge of the mountain. He stood at the right side of the clearing, looking out at the steep mountainside covered with rock shards and scraggly trees, and at the ocean below it all. When a rope was pulled some of the sun-warmed rainwater drizzled down from a huge showerhead. He rubbed soap over his muscles that were like rope.

After the shower he made himself a cup of strong coffee on his camp stove in the niche off the main room where he also kept the ancient icebox and the sink. He sat in his wobbly chair by the table and drank the black coffee slowly as he turned anything perplexing from the previous day over again and again in his mind, trying to get a firm hold on it.

Next came the main part of the day: his walk. He kept his knotty wooden stick by the door. He always walked down the mountain to the beach on the quieter part of the island. It was very humid, but after living on the island for eleven years it didn't bother Victor much. Neither did the rain, when it came, unless it was an unusually bad storm.

He took different routes to the beach. If he was feeling lazy, he took the path that the tourists took. Some of them staggered along in their new hiking boots, with red faces and spreading wet spots under their arms. Victor would offer the ones who hadn't brought any water some of his, and answer their questions politely, but he never encouraged conversation.

Most often, though, he used his stick to strike out through the jungle. He never got lost, and he liked to see the way the plants grew in the spots where people didn't pass by often.

Victor always got to the beach just as the fishermen were coming in for the day. After taking a quick dip in the ocean, he helped them drag their boats up on the sand and listened to their stories about how their day had gone, and sometimes if the day's catch was particularly good and there were many overflowing nets on the boats, he shouldered one of them and struggled alongside the brawnier fishermen to the top of the beach where the fish were cleaned. The fishermen gave Victor the heads, any other scraps, and all the fish too small to sell at market.

There was a vegetable stand and a small store nearby where he bought a few pastries for his lunch and whatever else he needed that day. Food cans were stacked high on the metal shelves of the store, and there was a shrine to the Virgin Mary on one wall. Victor had known Luis and Maria, the couple who ran the store, for years, but he rarely talked to them except to say good day and comment on the weather.

Besides his table and chair, his hut had a candle stuck

on the table in a puddle of wax, a few philosophy books bound in maroon leather on an old wooden shelf above the table, the books soft from reading and re-reading, and a mat and a folded rough blanket on the dirt floor for sleeping. The hut had nothing on the wooden walls and no light at night other than candlelight.

Victor also kept a few photographs on the shelf in a grimy plastic sandwich bag. They were of his family and the girlfriend he had left behind in Venezuela. He didn't look at them often, and when he did, he wondered why he didn't throw them away. He couldn't remember the people in them clearly any more, and it seemed easier not to have them around at all. Still, something made him hang on to them.

He kept the hut swept clean. Everything was in its place and there were no stray emotions there, either. The room was small but he never felt suffocated or claustrophobic. He felt at ease when he moved around his room and the things in it.

On the rare occasions when Victor went down to the tourist side of the island, to have a browse in the bookstore or just to walk around watching people, he was overwhelmed by the rapid motion and the maelstrom of words being spoken, swirling and tossing, spinning round.

After Victor got back to his hut, he would sit outside in the clearing for about fifteen minutes before going inside to cook dinner and then read and think for the rest of the evening. Sometimes the rabbits and cats came up to him to be petted. Other times he just sat in the cool of the waning day.

Every two weeks or so the bushes below the shower shifted and the wild man came out on all fours. His eyes were bloodshot. A long black beard dangled almost to the ground and its strands were stuck together with something oily. The skin on his face was cracked and a layer of fine white dust lay over it.

Under it, he looked like most of the people on the island, with their flat, soft mouths and noses and their long bodies. He lurked and swayed and held out his hand, then dashed swiftly back into the trees. Victor brought out the stale bread and dried meat he kept for the wild man, then sat quietly and waited for him to emerge again, as he always did. Victor doled out a few pieces of bread and meat at a time, putting them in the blue ceramic dish by the door. The wild man grabbed them, ran and sat on his haunches while he crammed them into his mouth, then came back for more.

The wild man had been the reason behind one of the few times Victor had initiated a conversation with Luis and Maria in the store by the beach. He'd asked if they knew anything about him. They said he was the son of an island family. He had always been strange when growing up, twitchy and anxious. Then as a young man he had gone completely mad because he'd smoked too much weed, and now he couldn't be around people any more. His mother left food out for him, but he stayed in the jungle and only came to her house to eat what she had put out for him once a week or so. Maria was friendly with the wild man's mother, and she said that at first the mother had tried to get him to a doctor, but after a few years of unsuccessful struggle she let him be. She didn't call him by his name any more, and neither did anyone else. Most days he fended for himself; some days he went to other houses for food, but he always slept by himself in the jungle.

At first when the wild man had started coming to the hut, he wouldn't look directly at Victor. His red, swollen eyes darted away, not quite frightened, but reactive to the slightest things around him. Now, after years of Victor feeding him and sitting patiently, waiting until he was absolutely sure he had run off, the wild man sometimes met Victor's eyes for a few seconds at a time. There was no craziness or confusion there. Instead, there was clarity every time and Victor felt startled by the strong sense of recognition. It was something he hadn't felt for many years. He wasn't in love with the wild man, of course not, but he aroused in him a strong sense of familiarity and loyalty.

The wild man usually stayed for no more than thirty minutes altogether. After he bounded off into the vegetation, Victor always felt odd. The order of his day was thrown off balance. Not in a bad way. He sat and thought about the wild man. The image of him hovered in his mind, and the feelings it brought with it spread into his chest and down to his stomach.

After the wild man's visits he often found himself drawn to the tourist side of the island, where he sat in José's café with the red walls and ordered coffee and chocolate cake, and afterwards he wandered to the church at the top of the village square.

The heavy wooden door wasn't too difficult to push open, and inside the church the cool damp worked its way into his skin, soothing the sticky flush of the humidity. He walked into the main chamber, with its windows that reached up and up, and sat on one of the wooden benches. The light coming through the windows was soft and filtered. The wood of the bench he was sitting on felt familiar to his fingers, and he stroked it as he looked around at the place where so many people must have come over the years.

Victor sat there as a few other people came and went, for what might have been a long time or might have been a short time.

The priest always came over and tried to start a conversation, and that was when he always left.

CHATTERING

Time alone was hard to find in Alex's house. He timed his trips to the toilet so that he would have time to have a good look at himself in the mirror. Their house only had one bathroom, and most of the time if someone was there too long, the rest of the family would bang on the thin door wanting to get in. There was a split in one side of it where his brother Jordan had punched it in a fit of rage. Sometimes, while his mother was out working at the restaurant and his brothers were in the back yard or watching a movie on TV, he could have a long look at himself. The mirror had three metal-framed sections. The centre section was flat against the wall, but you could swing open the mirrors on the left and the right to get to the medicine cabinet behind them. Alex always looked at himself for a while, studying his face – his freckled cheeks, the mole on the side of the short bumpy nose that he hated, and his sad blue eyes – wondering who this person looking back at him was and how he could find out for sure. Then he brought his face up against the edge of the mirror on the right, the one without all the rust spots on the glass, and swung it around a little, so that he became a cone-headed ogre with one eye or a Medusa with spreading hair, two noses, a huge mouth, and two small, pinched eyes.

The only things to read in the house were bills his mother got sent in the mail. They watched a lot of television, Jordan stretched out on the maroon velour La-Z-Boy right in front of the TV and the rest of them on the old brown sofa. After she was done with her shift at the restaurant, Alex's mother put on her pink sweats and found her spot on the sofa so she could have her beers and watch the talk shows where people's problems were sorted out in half an hour. When his mother was at work and they weren't at school, Alex and his brothers fought over what to watch. The top contenders were usually sports, the sitcoms, cartoons, and MTV. Jordan was big and muscular, so he usually won and they all watched ESPN, switching over to the other stuff during the commercials. The room was dark, with a low ceiling, one small window that was at the wrong angle to catch any light, and a lamp on the table by the sofa. The wavering glare of the television illuminated them all.

Alex remembered when his mother's arms had been thin, but now there was rippled fat under them. Her body was flabby and she had freckles on the backs of her hands. Whenever she hauled herself off the brown couch, she left a trail of wadded-up tissues, gossip magazines, half-empty bags of sour cream and onion potato chips, candy wrappers, and empty beer cans behind her. She was always angry when she came home from work, at the crusted dishes in the sink, the overflowing kitchen trash can, at how many people were in the house. Other people's messiness irritated her much more than her own.

From when he was about nine, Alex often went for long walks on his own around the neighbourhood. The Denny's restaurant where his mother worked was a few blocks away from the house, and there was a playground in between, behind his school. He would stop there and play on the yellow swing set for a while. When the swing got to a certain point in the air, its chains jumped and buckled, and then he stopped swinging and let it slow down by itself. He dragged his feet in the dirt beneath the swing, deepening the ruts in the ground, and then after a while he would get up to go to the corner store for some candy. Sometimes he took coins from his mother's purse to buy his favourite sour candy, but otherwise he wore a big sweatshirt and slipped the candy into his sleeve when the man at the counter was talking on his phone. The candy made his teeth stick together, and he chewed it as he walked up to the dumpster that stood against the concrete-block wall behind the corner store. If nobody was around, he dragged over one of the plastic orange crates that were stacked next to the dumpster, stood on it, and pushed up the rubber cover of the dumpster to look inside. There were sometimes things to read in there, all kinds of things – people's cancelled cheques, business letters, personal letters, thick books with small print and fake leather covers, or romance novels with women in flowing dresses leaning back under strong brown men. Alex climbed inside and read everything there was for a while. From reading the business letters, he thought he would like to be a lawyer one day. Lawyers seemed to know what to do.

There were a few houses in the neighbourhood where doors were never locked. Alex knew this because he often tried doors on his walks. A few times he had been caught, but he lied and said he had been visiting a friend and had gone to the store on the way, and wasn't this his friend's house? There was one big house that he loved, a few blocks away from his house in an area where the people had much more money. A man lived alone there, and he was often away. He kept his spare key under a loose tile by the side of the house – Alex had seen him put it there once when he was walking by. If there was no car in the driveway and more than one newspaper by the front door, Alex went inside. There were always expensive chocolates wrapped in gold foil in the refrigerator, and the clothes were all in plastic wrappers from the dry cleaners, hanging neatly in the closet. First white shirts, then blue ones, then all the other ones, and then pants. The shoes were ordered by colour, too, and the ties were on a rack. There were no women's clothes anywhere. He was sure the man lived alone.

In the living room the carpet was white and fluffy, with not a spot anywhere on it, and the man had a soft black leather couch in front of a big TV. He had a shower and a tub in his bathroom, with matching frosted bottles lined up at the sides. Alex had taken a bath in the tub once, squeezing a little from all of the bottles into the hot water. He hadn't dared stay in the bath too long – you never knew when the man was coming back, although there were only two newspapers at the front door so far. For as long as Alex had been watching the house, the man always stayed away at least five or six days.

Alex had looked in the desk, too. From a contract he found out that the man's name was Matthew Joseph and he was a lawyer. There were no personal letters or photographs there though, or anything that told Alex more about the lawyer and what he thought about when he was at home. There were notes about a case on a yellow pad in his handwriting, which was spiky and narrow. On the silver refrigerator was just one magnet, from a real-estate company.

At home their refrigerator was covered with magnets. One said 'It's either the house or me that's clean', and another one had a psalm on it. Alex was always careful to put everything in Matthew Joseph's house back the way he found it, although he sometimes ate a chocolate if there were enough in the refrigerator that he thought one wouldn't be easily missed.

Alex became a lawyer. He had worked as a waiter to pay his way through school. He bought a white carpet like the one in Matthew Joseph's house. Every place he lived had a big bathtub like Matthew Joseph's. He had some things that Matthew Joseph hadn't – a grand piano, that he kept by his front window. Matthew Joseph hadn't had many books, and Alex had hundreds of books on different subjects. He shelved them by category and then alphabetized them by author. He had read most of them too.

At parties, a glass of champagne was never missing from his hand, and he sipped it throughout the evenings. He saw many of the same people at these parties. There was a woman Alex liked to look at, with nervous grey eyes and red lipstick, and a large but beautiful body. She stood with her shoulders back, always in silky dresses and diamonds or simple black beads, and she had freckles on her tan chest. Her husband was short and jittery and always kept one skinny arm around her waist. He was the one with something to say. His wife would just ask how Alex had been.

Another woman, dark and wiry with big teeth that rose up into her swollen red gums, always wore bright turquoise or amber beads around her neck and long skirts. She talked about her most recent travels and how much nicer people were in other places. Alex didn't travel much, but he asked her about the historical landmarks and culture in the places she had visited, and what they were like. After a few minutes, he excused himself and moved to another cluster of people. They were all men this time, talking about business and which stocks to buy.

Alex was polite to everyone. People came and went.

His brother Jordan called him sometimes to ask for money, and Alex gave it to him. He got angry though, and often told Jordan to stop pestering him for god's sakes.

Lately a woman Alex had seen at parties for years was trying to get him to join her group that met once a month for the members to talk about themselves. Their childhoods, their relationships, the books they read and what that said about them. Michelle wasn't at all pretty, but she had convinced herself that she was. She had big hips and a big nose, with dyed short blonde hair, and her fingernails were always perfectly painted. She would lay her hands with their glistening nails lightly on people's shoulders when she talked to them and look into their eyes for a long time. She moved around rooms purposefully. She chose whom she wanted to talk to and what should be said. She had decided that Alex should be her friend. Alex wasn't sure if he wanted to be, but it would probably be easier to just give in to her. For the time being he was still holding out, though.

Michelle always exclaimed to him how so very interesting he was because he'd read and seen everything that she brought up. She often sent him some article or other she liked and asked his opinion on it. She said his replies were revealing psychologically and she wanted to discuss them with him the next time they met. She was always inviting him out to dinner or to Sunday lunch. Alex never went.

One weekend, though, he decided to go. He hadn't been out all weekend and he wanted a distraction. He drove to her house, chewing gum. The sun was shining and he found the place easily. The guard in his little enclosure at the entrance into the gated community smiled as he waved Alex in. Michelle's orange-pink Spanish-style house with its adobe roof tiles was at one end of a cul-de-sac and had a twisted iron railing by the concrete steps leading up to it. He rang the doorbell, and when Michelle let him into the white hallway he saw pieces by artists he knew on the walls. He was surprised to see that he was the only person in the house, even though he was twenty minutes late. She said she'd forgotten to tell him that the lunch had been delayed. He followed her into the living room.

The glasses were placed rim down, lined up exactly with the stripes in the white-on-white silk tablecloth. Two rows of stripes separated each glass from the next one. There were sixteen glasses all together, four down and four across, and the forks were in two rows, just so, next to them. The knives were next to the forks. White linen napkins were folded on the diagonal and plumped in a silver basket next to the crystal vase of mixed pink flowers.

She asked him if he wanted some champagne while they waited for the other guests, and poured two glasses out, handing one to him. They sat on the white sofa. Alex noticed that on her side of the sofa was a trail, just like his mother always left behind. Michelle's trail was tissues, sunglasses, lipstick, mints, and a few fashion magazines. She began to show him a few books spread out on the coffee table that she said she particularly wanted his view on.

He gave her his views.

He wondered why the books he had read in the dumpster had drawn him in so much more than any since then.

One of the partners at Alex's law firm came into his mind. The man had recently gone AWOL. Nobody knew where he was, not even his ex-wife and children. Word was that he had gone to Mexico with his new girlfriend to avoid being taken to court over the divorce. Alex knew the man as a pretty arrogant son of a bitch, but it was still surprising to think of him hiding away from his own children. He had been the highest-earning partner at the firm.

Alex decided firmly, then and there, not to join Michelle's group. It was a gut response. He didn't know why it had come at that moment, but it had.

They talked for a while longer about the books, Michelle saying how astute Alex was as she placed her hand on his shoulder.

The lunch went as he had expected. No surprises. Nice food, nice champagne, nice chat. He made his excuses and left as soon as he politely could.

Alex went to the gym during his lunch hour if he didn't have too much work. If it was sunny and he couldn't face going to the gym, he often went to the patch of green in front of his office block with a sandwich from the deli, and found a bench. Today, he was sitting there with a ham sandwich and a Coke. Sometimes he watched people, but today, after he'd finished eating, he closed his eyes and let the sun fall on his face.

Suddenly he felt a hand on his shoulder. He opened his eyes and saw that it was Michelle. She had shopping bags in her hands – the smart shops weren't too far away from the firm. He hadn't seen her for some time. He greeted her and she sat down next to him, exclaiming how long it had been since they'd seen each other, and saying he had to come to lunch on Sunday, and had he seen this particularly interesting exhibition yet?

He smiled and answered pleasantly. The partner from the law firm had been making an appearance in his mind again, along with the dumpster. He wasn't sure why.

Suddenly, he took Michelle's hand in his, pulled

her towards him and bit down on her bare forearm, hard. The warm flesh gave way under his teeth and it had a nice texture. When he let go Michelle had red tooth marks on her arm. He smiled at her as if it were a perfectly everyday thing to do. She smiled back at him.

'I have a lot of work to do Sunday, but if I finish in time I'll come to your lunch,' he told her. 'See you then.'

Dismissed, she walked away, looking at her arm with a fixed smile on her face. Alex felt a bit bad. It wasn't really the thing to do, biting people. But it sure had shut her up, and it felt good. He sat back, closed his eyes, and let the sun fall on him again.

The disappearance of the partner meant that there was even more work to do than usual. The secretaries filled cardboard cartons with files from the partner's office and wiped the coffee rings from his desk. The partner's endless cups of coffee had seemed an ingrained part of the firm's character, but some extra-strength cleanser soon got rid of them. The few gold-framed personal photos on his desk were thrown away and the boxes of files brought to Alex and the other lawyers who had been assigned to take up the slack.

They stayed late every night for weeks.

Every night the building gradually went dark except for three squares of yellow light, each on a different floor. One was Alex's office, third from the left on the fourth floor; another was the centre office on the seventh floor; and the third was the very last office on the right on the top floor.

When he worked through the night, Alex occasionally bumped into one of the others by the free coffee machine. The lattes, cappuccinos, and plain coffee from the machine all tasted exactly the same, thick with artificial sweetener. The mixture tasted like the instant hot chocolate powder he had eaten as a kid, with a spoon, straight from the box, when his mother was waiting for her pay cheque and there was no food in the house. It coated his tongue in the same way and stuck to the back of his throat.

Walking back to his office from the coffee machine, he sometimes stopped by the big window by the elevator; there was one on each floor of the building. He liked looking out on the night.

He remembered the time he had climbed a high tree, when he was about eight. He had grasped each thick bough tightly and climbed up and up. Nobody else had been around – it was just him and the tree. The snow was dirty on the ground. When he got to the top, the branch was suddenly thin and bendy compared with the ones below. It broke when he hoisted himself up on it and he went crashing down, twigs and branches scratching his face and arms as he fell through them, a big one scraping his back roughly as he slid down it. He hit the ground and felt the snow melting through his jacket, prickling the big scrape on his back. It hurt and he lay there, but then he got up and walked home. Nobody asked what had happened, and he hadn't told anybody about it.

THE PIRATES

E ven at night, the dolphins were visible beneath the waves. Every few hours he saw the pearly white shapes at the sides of the boat, beautifully distorted through the water. They swam along like that for a while. It felt like they were biding their time. Then they broke the surface. A few leaps, and they changed positions, swimming down under the boat and up the other side, jumping into the air ahead. They led the way, playing with each other. After switching sides three or four times, they seemed to get bored and swam off.

Other than the dolphins, the moon was their only companion during those night watches. When it was full, it pushed the darkness to the edges of the horizon. When there was no moon, the night was black and quiet and the boat was alone in the middle of the ocean under the scattering of stars. A breeze sometimes started up around midnight, and then Tony brought up a blue wool blanket and wrapped himself in it. He let the night wash over him.

They had oatmeal every day for breakfast, and for

lunch and dinner they had the fish that he or, less often, she killed with a spear and cooked over coals on the small black barbecue on the deck. Sometimes when they were in shallow waters, off an island, they dived to the bottom and brought up conches. They cracked the gnarled shells with a hammer and picked out the fragments from the pink muscle inside, then chucked it onto the barbecue. It was thicker and meatier than the delicate white flesh of the fish they caught. Sometimes they had lemons to squeeze onto the fish, or some hot chillies and garlic to put on top as it grilled.

They had been hoping to get back to the mainland within a week or two, but the wind was against them, so they would be at sea or docked off the islands for at least another month, probably more. There was a bottomless supply of fish, though, and plenty of oatmeal. When they were hot or dirty, which was most of the time, they dived overboard and swam. Their hair was thick and dreadlocked with salt. The sun was strong. She wanted a freshwater shower badly, and so did he, but he minded not having one less.

Each island they sailed past was different. One had a smart restaurant with windows open to the ocean and only two tables. The richer tourists paid for a boat taxi from Nassau to eat there. Another of the islands was jointly owned by the cruise ship companies. Americans and their pasty-skinned children plastered in sun block would be boated over for a taste of jungle paradise and a barbecue to boot. Many of the islands they passed were completely deserted, or just had a shop and a few houses on them where Bahamian fishermen lived. One had the ruins of an old mansion. The Bahamians who worked on the cruise ship island had told Tony that the mansion had once been owned and defended by a Caribbean gangster and gambler, and he wanted to see its remains. He never knew how Rebecca would react when he told her what he was thinking. Sometimes she was generous, and at other times she was dismissive. He knew he was the same towards her. But this time when he asked her if she would like to go ashore to see the mansion, she nodded and got up from her book.

Once he got the boat close enough to the island, he jumped out and waded through the warm shallows to the beach, where there was an old wooden pillar. Rebecca threw out the rope to him. As Tony wrapped the wet rope around the post, it squelched and dripped water as he knotted it, and he felt her eyes on his back.

He held out his arm to help her jump down from the boat. She had thin fingers and her grasp was light as she put her weight on him for a few seconds as she stepped off. He liked it.

They could see what was left of the mansion from the beach as they slogged side by side through the hot sand. He told her what he had heard about the owner, the legendary poker games and his eventual downfall.

Some of the brown weeds that grew on the island

brushed against their legs and scratched them as they neared the mansion. The ruins were crusted with moss. Bright green lizards darted in and out of the cracks in the thick, broken-down walls. Tony and Rebecca tramped over the concrete blocks and bent metal rods that were left over from the building. After half an hour, they went back to the boat. Rebecca didn't let Tony help her back into the boat. She walked through the water ahead of him and pulled herself up the ladder and onto the deck. He felt no eyes on his back as he undid the ropes and pushed the boat off.

In the two months Rebecca had been on the boat they had barely exchanged more than a few words, and they touched even less than they talked, but he thought that she could feel most of his mood shifts. He was either at the wheel or looking out on the changeable sea. It was most often calm, the waves regular and small, but he was not complacent.

Most of the time he was naked. It was rare that they came close to an inhabited island, but when they did he pulled on a pair of blue Hawaiian swimming trunks. If they were going ashore, then he had a T-shirt from a surf shop back home in Kingston, full of holes, and orange flip-flops, but that was all. Rebecca was always in her black bikini. She was shy around him, never mind that he had seen her straining into the red plastic bucket and throwing the contents overboard just the morning after they first met.

For going ashore she had cut-off jean shorts and a thin green tank top, or a short purple-striped dress. She too had only flip-flops to put on her feet. Hers were black, like the old tyres lying around on the islands.

The boat, *My Girl*, wasn't a big boat. Tony had bought it dilapidated and fixed it up. Rebecca slept right by the wooden ladder leading to the hold in a narrow bunk with a navy blue sleeping bag spread on it. The sleeping bag got sticky in the heat, so most nights she lay on top of it, sweating.

If he craned his neck while he was lying in his bed he could just glimpse her outline. She slept curled up tight like a child, her brown hair twisted on the pillow and her long body awkward in repose, the opposite of most people he had secretly watched while they were sleeping. All the parts of their disjointed personalities and bodies that he puzzled over in the day usually came together in sleep.

Tony slept in the back of the boat, on a big bed with proper sheets. There was just the deck above and the ladder leading down to Rebecca's bunk, with the sink opposite, and above that the cabinet where he stored the dried food. Beside the cabinet were the water bottles stacked one on top of another. Past that the walls narrowed gradually to a point, and his bed fitted into that space. Rebecca had never even sat on the edge of his bunk. He told himself that she thought it would be an invasion of his privacy. It was his boat after all and she was a guest on it.

127

They often went for days without seeing anyone. Rebecca helped him with the sailing when he needed her to, pulling the ropes that he told her to pull and ducking when the boom came swinging over to the other side. They swam. The sun lulled them almost into another state of consciousness, raised delicately above the old fractured one. Sometimes the balance shifted and the sun made them feel too hot, and nauseous with it, but then they jumped overboard. The sky was clear and bright blue. Occasionally, a cloud passed overhead. It had not rained once in all their time at sea.

The air smelled of salt.

When Tony thought of big cities full of tangled issues and people bustling along on the streets it seemed like a sci-fi movie about the overtaking of the planet Earth. Rebecca did crossword puzzles and read novels they had got from people they'd met at one of the bigger islands.

At night, he consulted his maps and decided where was safest to drop anchor. The boat rocked to and fro and the clouds drifted over the moon. Rebecca sat on the bench near the wheel and looked out on the sea, while he took his Jack Daniel's and sat in the bow, drinking from the bottle and brooding. After a few hours, Rebecca would come over to say good night before going down to bed. He usually went down an hour or two after she did.

When they first met, Tony had asked Rebecca where she came from and how she had happened to be at the

dock in Nassau looking for work as crew. Then he told
her how he made the decision to strike out in *My Girl*.
They had laughed softly together, they had sat side by
side on the deck under the moon. Even as Tony wanted
to let the feeling from that night rest deep down in himself, he couldn't. He had a live awareness of the frail,
unidentifiable sensation that had passed through his
chest. But now they simply circled around each other,
each thinking their own thoughts. He got angry sometimes. Shouldn't they have had sex by now? Was he that
undesirable? But then again he hadn't made a move on
her either. He wasn't shy, but it was something about
their surroundings. It was funny, if he'd thought about
it beforehand, alone on a boat in the middle of the
ocean with a girl – of course they couldn't help but be
shagging all the time. But now that he was on the boat
with Rebecca, even the idea of sex felt different. Sex
couldn't be consolation that he could forget about when
the girl left.

Tony's hand found the curve of Rebecca's waist often,
just in passing on the small boat, and always it felt somehow familiar. He had watched it long enough, as she lay
with a book on the deck of the boat. Ostensibly he
watched the sea, or talked with other sailors on the
shortwave radio, making sure the boat stayed on its
course, but he couldn't help his eyes straying. He
thought hers did too, but he couldn't be sure. The isolation was complete and the enclosing heat lazy and

smooth. Every gesture and word was heightened, but slipped away too quickly.

For two months it had been sunny. But one night, just as they dropped anchor, the rain started. A few drops at first, and then more rain came, until it was a full-blown storm. The humidity gathered under the rain so that it pressed down on them, and the ocean smashed all around the boat, lifting it up high and then dropping it straight down with a boom. The wind picked up the rain and blew it across so that it blinded Tony. The anchor was secure, but they didn't feel like they were. They clutched hands and felt their way through the beating rain over to the hatch, scrambled down the ladder, threw it down, and fixed the wooden board in its slots so that they were shielded from the weather, but there were leaks and the air was heavy with moisture. Rebecca's bed was soaked, so they would both have to sleep in Tony's bed. She lay down on the left edge of the bed, and Tony lay on the opposite side. He had two sheets, so they had one apiece. The boat rode the storm as best she could. Rebecca fell asleep and Tony stared at the low ceiling. After a long while he fell asleep too.

When he felt her hands on him, guiding him inside her, he was still half-asleep. The air was muggier than ever and the accumulated layers of salt, sweat and dirt that had once felt protective now just made him feel smelly and filthy. His eyes were glued shut with sand and humidity, and yet he was inside her. The smell of her blended with the viscous smell of the sea and the rain around them. They didn't kiss. It didn't last long, but the whole of their bodies pressed tightly and warmly together and his chin fitted into her shoulder as she moved on him. Afterwards, he fell asleep again and when he awoke in the morning he couldn't know with any certainty that it had happened. The sea was calm, and Rebecca was already up and cooking their oatmeal in her black bikini. She nodded a good morning like she did every morning. Maybe she was somewhat more reluctant to meet his eyes, but he didn't know for sure.

The day went much as usual. Tony talked on the shortwave to other sailors about the storm. None of the boats he was in regular communication with had been lost, everyone was okay and the weather forecast was good. They were due to come to an island that day, for the first time in a while. He worked out their course and stayed on it. The moisture in the air was drying up fast, but the waves were still restless. There was wreckage strewn on the surface of the water – branches, fish float-ing belly-up, dead birds, old tyres and pieces of plastic tubing. Rebecca bustled around the boat, tidying up and drying down. He watched her and wondered whether it had really happened.

They came to the island and Rebecca, in her bikini top and shorts, jumped onto the dock to wrap the line around one of the piles and knot it. Tony was more eager than usual to be ashore, to see other people, to be away from the world of the boat. The island had a wooden counter under a metal awning; it sold beer and rum and Cokes. There was a small store, a few ramshackle fishing boats riding low in the water at the dock, and a dirt road leading to a cluster of houses. He headed for the bar, as did Rebecca. There were a few fishermen there, and he gossiped with them about the storm. The cold beer broke through the dusty stale taste of the past few days as it went down his throat. Rebecca was talking with another fisherman in the corner, leaning against the peeling turquoise counter.

'Hey, Tony!' she said.

'What?'

'This guy's going over to Nassau today – his boat can make it even without the wind, his engine's strong enough. Think I might go with him. D'you mind? My friend's getting married soon, like I told you, and here's a chance to make the wedding.'

'Yeah, sure, okay, if that's what you want.'

She went to get her stuff from *My Girl*, and he went to help her. She had one backpack, but he carried it for her. The two fishermen on the boat that was taking her to Nassau wore only underpants that drooped at the crotch. Their eyes looked dodgy, but what the hell, it wasn't up to him. Their boat dragged in the water. Rebecca sat on the floor surrounded by ice chests filled with fish and held on to a rope attached to the bow as the bigger of the two men pumped up the outboard engine. She waved goodbye to Tony as the boat gathered speed.

The wake from the boat stretched long towards the island.

Tony ordered a double rum and Coke. He needed something stronger than a beer.

WINDOW WASHER

The house in Notting Hill had eight small clay sculptures laid out on black velvet beneath a glass case in the living room. The white mantel above the fireplace was crowded with thick, creamy, heavy cards. Christian peeked at them as he was cleaning the insides of the windows and saw that most of them had a printed Merry Christmas on them and then the name of the sender scrawled underneath, without any handwritten message. Some were party invitations, and others notices of art gallery openings.

The windows in this room took up most of one wall. They were just one sheet of glass each. Easy to clean.

Christian had cleaned the outsides of all the windows earlier. Now he used a razor blade to scrape off any tiny splotches of dirt from the glass. Then he soaped the windows, all the way down. The soapy water dripped over the glass and onto the wooden floor. He swished the squeegee across the top of the window in one smooth motion, then worked his way down and swooped across the other way, then down and across again. After he rubbed out any streaks with the rag and wiped the soap and water off the floor, he moved onto the next window, leaving the ones behind him clear and clean.

The owner of the house was a blonde woman whom Christian had never seen before that day. He was afraid to get a drop of water on her. Every hair on her head was in its place and the wet day didn't reach her. The bottoms of her jeans touched the floor, but even though she had gone out in the garden earlier to yank her dog back into the house, the edges of her trousers weren't wet or dirty. The cuffs of Christian's khaki cargo pants were wet and dirty, as well as frayed. He'd rolled them up at the bottom so that they didn't leave dirty spots on any of the furniture.

She moved around the rooms on the same floor while Christian worked, talking on her phone. Christian saw her glance into the gold-framed mirror above the fireplace, smoothing down her eyebrows with a forefinger. Then, still on the phone, she adjusted the knick-knacks and books in the room. The books were straight on the shelves next to the mantel, placed in decreasing order from biggest to smallest. A vase of red roses was moved so that it was perfectly in the middle of the coffee table. He watched her so he knew where she was. Some of the house owners were nit-picky, keeping an eye on him to make sure that he didn't get a speck of soap on their furniture, but they didn't want him hoisting his ladder up in their houses, either. When he saw the woman's reflection in the mirror as she walked up the stairs beyond the open door, he quickly laid a clean rag on top of her blue armchair and stood on its back to reach the top part of the window, then leapt off the chair as soon as he was finished.

He'd cleaned the windows in her bedroom earlier. There were no photographs anywhere. Two identical white robes hung on the back of the bathroom door, and not even one hair was in the sink or the shower. The toilet looked brand new. He wondered if they cleaned everything every time they used it.

When he was working, he often thought of people he had loved and not seen for a long time – his grandmother's close-lipped smile, or the green cat eyes of the first girl he had ever loved. He wondered if she was thinking about him that minute too.

When he remembered them, strange remnants of feelings tightened in his chest, but he couldn't easily identify them the way he could the images. Most of the time it was just an unsettling wondering.

His thoughts preoccupied him and he often forgot that anyone was around him. When the owner of the house tapped him on the shoulder and motioned 'Drink?' it startled him and he gave a little jump. It took a moment for him to come back to where he was. Then he nodded and smiled.

—Yes, tea, please, thank you. He acted as if he were milking a cow's teat with his hand to tell her 'milk' and held up one finger to tell her he wanted a sugar.

People sometimes brought biscuits. Not this time. But when he took a sip of the tea it was sweet and reassuring.

Christian was surprised when the owner stayed in the room with a cup of tea of her own. It did happen sometimes in the smaller flats, but never before in this kind of house. He noticed that his tea was in a mug with the phone numbers of an insurance company on the side and hers was in a white porcelain cup.

She sat on the arm of the chair Christian had stood on earlier and straightened her legs, as thin as a teen's in their jeans and ballet slippers. There was a tortoiseshell hairclip on the coffee table and she shook her smooth hair out then pinned it back into a swirl with the clip. He stayed standing – somehow it didn't feel right to him to sit down in her house, even if he was on his tea break.

She pointed to the sculptures in their case and then to her pink lips. He saw on them 'Can you read my lips?'

He could understand those words, but he often couldn't follow longer conversations, so he shook his head and motioned for a pen and paper. When she brought these back from the kitchen, he saw that she had written in thick, smooth black ink, 'These sculptures are about the voice and silence. What do you think about that?' She pointed to the case as Christian read.

What did he think about that? He had no idea. The sculptures looked like wormy lumps of clay to him.

He didn't know this woman. She had given him tea in a different sort of cup to hers.

Christian thought for a time about what to say to her. Finally, he shrugged and took the pen from her to write, 'I not think anything about it. Thanks for the tea.'

When he was done with the windows, Christian loaded the squeegee and sponge into his bucket; the rags went in his black athletic bag, and then he brought everything to the front door while he waited to get paid before driving on to the next place. It had stopped raining, so he leaned against the front of the house. The woman had been pacing back and forth in her big kitchen, muttering busily into her tiny mobile phone. She had so many people to talk to. She held up a finger at him to hold on.

When she was finally ready to pay, she haggled over the money, searching around in her white leather handbag and then holding out a ten-pound note and a few pound coins. Christian shook a finger at her. Twenty pounds was what they had agreed, and that was that. She shook her head and patted his shoulder a few times. The veins in her throat stood out, green and purple. Finally she pulled out a twenty-pound note and gave it to him. The strained smile on her face was one that Christian saw often on adults' faces when they smiled at children. He didn't like it.

Most of the other flats he cleaned windows at were in north London, and since he'd started doing this work he had got to know all the side streets and cut-throughs when driving between jobs. His small car swerved to pass the cars parked tightly along the streets. He absentmindedly wiped the dust from the dashboard with one hand as he drove, and removed a pen from the ashtray, where he kept them. He might need it for the next flat in Archway, because he'd never been there before or met the owner.

Christian had posted up flyers offering his window-cleaning and decorating services in off-licence windows all over town and slipped them under doors and windscreen wipers. Looking at the texts on his mobile, he found the one from the man about how to get to his flat.

He parked outside the building, then pressed the button of flat number 2, tapping on the intercom. The man was expecting him at this time. He rattled the door handle till the door gave way, then walked down the hall to the flat.

The man standing in the doorway had bags under his eyes and his skin looked bruised and grey. He knew Christian was deaf because he'd put it on the flyer next to his phone number, so the man mouthed exaggeratedly, 'Do all the windows, inside and outside.' He pointed at the windows, and then went into another room and shut the door without asking Christian if he understood.

Christian went to do the outside windows first, leaving both the door to the flat and the one into the building propped open just a crack. There were whitish deposits of limescale crusted like bird shit over the entire panes, not just at the sides near the frame as they usually were. The windows were made up of many small panels, so that made it harder, too. He had to scrape them for an hour before washing them. His knuckles were red and sore from scraping for so long in the cold air.

Occasionally the scraping was interrupted by someone walking by on the pavement – an old lady in a navy-and-red-striped headscarf with a small terrier, or a young mother in sweatpants and a matching hoodie with her little girl. Christian saw them coming out of the corner of his eye and turned his head from his work for just long enough to smile at them, but they didn't smile back.

After finishing outside, he went back into the building and on into the flat to do the windows inside. He could work his way more quickly through the kitchen and the living room because there was not nearly as much limescale there. Inside the flat it was filthy. There was no furniture. The *Sun* and the racing papers were strewn all over the living-room floor. Boxes with pictures of appliances on their sides were stacked by the walls, filled with papers, books, framed pictures, old toys, rubbish. Christian glanced over them quickly. He would have liked to study the objects this man saved more closely, but he didn't want to seem nosy. There was a heavy, sour smell in the air. The man was still in the room he had entered after letting Christian in, which Christian assumed was the bedroom.

It was odd to Christian that this man wanted his windows cleaned when there was so much else happening in his flat that needed attention. But it wasn't for Christian to ask.

It was awkward when he knocked on the door to the bedroom. He wasn't sure if the man wanted the window in there to be cleaned, but he needed to get paid anyway. When the man opened the door, he beckoned Christian into the dark room and pushed him towards the one blanket-covered window. The room was lit with candlelight. Christian could make out posters of the Hindu elephant god, Jesus, and the Last

Supper plastered over one wall, with tea lights lined up at the base of the wall. The man was on his knees by the tea lights, bowing from the waist repeatedly. His mouth was moving but Christian didn't know what he was saying.

He lifted the blanket covering the window, an old flowered pink quilt, to clean the glass underneath. The quilt was so heavy that it resisted Christian's efforts to roll it up or push it all to one side, and it flopped over his head as he did the window. He couldn't see what the man was doing. He didn't know if he was glad or a little curious. He had to get on with his job, but he wasn't as careful as usual.

After he finished, he saw that the man was still kneeling. He shook the man's shoulder and motioned for money. The man pointed out to the hallway and gestured to Christian to go there, rubbing his thumb against his forefingers in the universal sign for money. Walking to the door, Christian saw a crumpled twenty-pound note on a chair in the short corridor, on top of some Chinese-takeaway flyers.

He let himself out of the flat and breathed in the air outside. The dirty London air felt clean compared with the air inside that flat. Christian was hungry. There was a fried-chicken restaurant he often went to near Archway station, so he drove there and fed enough coins into the meter to have the time to heave out a proper breath over lunch.

At the counter, he pointed at the pictures on the mat next to the cash register to order his usual fried-chicken burger, chips and Coke. He sat at the Formica table under the fluorescent lights, tearing open the plastic packets of ketchup and the paper ones of salt for his chips.

The man at the table in front of him, eating the same kind of chicken burger, had on a neon pink hoodie and matching hat pulled down over his ears. A newspaper lay on the table in front of him, next to his food. He stayed on the same page for a very long time, the one with a picture of a girl with only panties on, smiling coyly at the camera as she held one arm to her breasts.

Christian looked out of the window beyond the man and his newspaper into the street. The glass was spattered with dirt thrown up from passing cars and needed cleaning – maybe he would ask the manager of the restaurant if he wanted him to clean it. But it wasn't so dirty that Christian couldn't see the people on the pavement. Some were alone, but most were with other people. There was a pretty girl with a blonde ponytail in an army jacket, athletic pants with three stripes down the side, and trainers, walking hand in hand with her boyfriend, who was dressed the same way. The boyfriend whispered in her ear, and she smiled up at him.

If he had a voice, he sure could kill a hell of a lot of

time. That was what Christian should have said to that woman in the house in Notting Hill, he thought, as he dabbed his chip in the puddle of ketchup and put it into his mouth.

THE DEAF
SCHOOL

The deaf school had originally been in beautiful old buildings up in the mountains with dark green tiles lining the marbled archways and courtyards, and fountains in the centre of each of the three squares. But the hearing students at the nearby university needed more buildings, more room, more of everything. The beautiful old school tempted them, so they found a way to take it over for themselves.

The deaf school had to move a few hours away, to a town bordered by dry brown hills. Fast-food restaurants were everywhere. There wasn't much else there. The new school was made up of near-identical buildings that looked like the houses in a Monopoly game.

The buildings were painted a sludgy brown, with orange carpet inside and squat dormitories for the children to sleep in.

Many deaf adults moved to the town, too. As children they'd gone to the old school in the mountains, and they went where the school went. They worked at the school, mostly in the dormitories as house parents, and their children went to classes there. The school was where the sporting events with other deaf schools or deaf clubs were held, and where the graduates who hadn't found jobs and were living off government hand-outs would gather in the parking lot by the gymnasium, to deal drugs, flirt, gossip, or tell stories. The deaf children often had birthday parties in the student activity centre, and their weddings, wedding-anniversary parties, and baby showers would be there too. It was one of the only places for miles around where they could be sure of communication with the people around them.

Ally was one of the children in the first class at the new school. She had already been living in the town with her hearing parents when they found out she couldn't hear. Both of them had grown up in the town – it was just a strange kind of good luck that their daughter had turned out to be deaf. They were nice people. The mother always wore bright pink lipstick, heavy mascara on the lashes around her small eyes, and purple, pink or mauve flowered dresses. Her lips were pointy and narrow. She ordinarily pressed them fixedly together, but when she saw some of the children who Ally went to school with, she would bend over, open her bright pink mouth wide, and say a very big 'HELLO! HOW ARE YOU?' whilst fluttering her eyelashes. Then she would smile tightly and nod abruptly, before doing a small sashay and walking off again. She learned a bit of sign language, but her signs were stiff, awkward, and small, her face never altering its hard expression as she signed, so the children found her difficult to understand. They never really had long conversations with her and it appeared she preferred it that way. She never asked them why they seemed not to understand her. She would adjust the black knob in her ear that was almost always there. It connected her to her music. Then she would smile tightly.

She behaved the same way with the deaf adults. She would say a brief hello to them when she came to one of Ally's school things. Ally's father was warmer and more relaxed, but he also was not very inclined towards conversation and was always busy with work or whatever else he was involved with.

Ally was one of the lucky ones, though, because she could ask her parents for whatever she needed or wanted – food, water, help with her homework, toys, or anything else, and she could read and write much better than most of the other children at the school. Her classmate Ray had joined the class at the same time she had, but he couldn't say anything to anyone other than 'Food' and 'Pee'. He would cup his groin with a small hand and jerk upwards to show the teacher that he had to go to the bathroom, or he would open his mouth with its perpetual cold sores around the lower left corner and stuff his fingers into it to tell the teacher that he was hungry. Other than that he would sit on his chair by his plastic desk with its fake-wood veneer and open and close his mouth, over and over again. His lower jaw was a bit wider and longer than his upper, so his face always looked muscular and wide. He was good at sports and had a mysterious way of understanding the rules of basic games like Four Square, where you tossed a ball around and around, allowing only one bounce per person. When break time came he would be the first to run out to the playground and join in one of the games.

Later, in a few years' time, when he had picked up some more words and language, he would reveal a sweet and strong personality, always asking everyone how they were when they came back from weekends with their families, never missing one person. But for the first few years, he just sat opening and closing his mouth. His eyes wandered over everything and everyone, never remaining anywhere specific for long.

The teachers had tried to talk to Ray's parents to find out more about him, but Ray's parents said they didn't have the time to talk to anyone. They were hearing and didn't know any sign language. They said they just didn't want to have to support Ray his entire life and that was all. Other than that, they were already busy enough, they said. Nobody had ever gone with Ray to his house on the weekends, although, much later on, Ray was always looking around to go over to someone else's house, somewhere where they knew a bit more sign language and could talk to him.

He would ask question after question of the friend's

parents. How had they met? Where – in which town? How long ago? What did they do to earn money? How did they decide on that job? How long did they have to go to school? Did they like it? What did they tend to do on the weekends? Did they do it together or separately? How did they decide what to do? What were they having for dinner? How were they going to cook it? Why? He would open and shut his mouth in that definite flat way of his in between the questions, a habit from those first few years that would stay with him for the rest of his life.

He was always very helpful and sweet, but sometimes he would erupt, flailing around with his arms and legs and then huddling into a corner with his lower jaw sticking out, shaking his head and refusing to talk to anyone for hours and hours. Eventually he would come out of it and apologize and be back to normal.

The teachers talked amongst themselves about whether Ray would be one of the graduates who sold drugs and flirted in the parking lot and lived on government handouts. It was very possible, but maybe he had come to the school early enough to be able to go on to vocational school at least.

Joey and Sophie would watch the teachers talking about Ray. They were the only two in the class who had deaf parents. Sophie's parents had gone to the deaf university and worked at the school, too; Joey's hadn't gone to college, but they knew Sophie's parents from the deaf sports circuit – Sophie's father and Joey's father had played on the same basketball team a few times.

Sophie was very shy, but Joey loved to tell stories. He could sign beautifully. He was tall and thin, with long arms and wide, long fingers, and when he told the rest of the class stories, his arms would become whatever he was telling the story about. One of his favourite stories, learned from one of his many older brothers, was about a racing car speeding around tight curves, flames shooting out from below the car as it flew over gulfs and canyons. His arms would become the car itself, speeding up so fast that it defied gravity, flying, and then braking sharply to a stop. He would show the rest of them how the driver's hair was plastered against his skull by air pressure as the car flew over abysses, and how his eyes squinted shut against the bits of gravel coming at them. Joey telling a story was almost better than a movie, because you could see and feel the emotion and the physical sensations on his face and body, as you couldn't really see and feel in movies. Sophie loved to read but she never saw anything in any book to equal one of Joey's stories.

They would all ask him again and again for more stories, especially Ray. Ray could always follow Joey's stories, even at the very beginning. His favourite was the one where Joey told them about doing a slam dunk, the basketball player leaping up high, the muscles in his legs pulsing, to grab the rim of the basket firmly, eyes bulging, mind rejoicing, legs and whole body dangling until finally he let go and came back down to earth.

Sophie loved Joey's stories too, but she didn't like the way the teachers talked about Ray. The teachers were mostly hearing, and some of them signed even worse than Ally's bright-pink-lipped mother, sloppily and choppily. They were difficult to watch or follow and the children would get very tired from seeing them sign. Many times Sophie and Joey had to tell them the same thing again and again and sign very slowly for the teachers to understand them, and even then they would just smile tightly back and nod. Often Sophie didn't say anything in class just because she didn't want to have to go through it again with the teachers. It was an awkward, heavy feeling for her.

Ally, who signed to the teachers the same way she signed to her mother, was the teachers' favourite.

Sometimes, when Ray was watching Joey tell a story during class, the teachers would stride over and sign impatiently to Joey to stop that nonsense and jerk Ray around to face them again. Sophie could see that Ray couldn't understand anything the teachers were saying, but that he loved Joey's stories so much and understood them. She got angry when the teachers did that to him, but of course they didn't care what she thought. They would keep writing words on the blackboard and spelling them out to Ray, who just sat there opening and shutting his mouth with its protruding lower jaw, occasionally looking over to Joey in the hope that another story might have begun.

Once a week they went for speech lessons. Joey and Ally were partners for the lessons, and Ray and Sophie went together. The speech teacher was an old lady who always smelled slightly too sweet. She had a small toy monkey that would climb up a tower if you could keep your voice at the same level for long enough, and she would hold up a thin layer of Kleenex tissue and ask you to say 'b' and 'p'. With the 'p', the Kleenex was supposed to blow out and with the 'b', it wasn't supposed to. She held one hand up to Sophie's throat to feel her saying 'bat' and 'pat'. Sophie tried her best at the speech lessons but she just couldn't get the hang of it. Her younger sister had more hearing than she did and she was very good at speech. Sophie was a bit jealous because it meant her younger sister had a way to get their parents to buy her more things – music tapes, or a cassette player.

Ray was also better than she was at speech, though – maybe it was because he had hearing parents. He always made the monkey go up the tower and stay there for quite some time, and at the end of the lessons he would have a bigger stack than Sophie did of the scratch-and-sniff stickers that the speech teacher gave out as rewards. The speech teacher would tell Sophie how it was very sad that she wasn't good at speech, because it meant she wouldn't be able to communicate with hearing people

who didn't understand sign language, or get a job with
hearing people in the future. She would have to work
at the deaf school like her parents.

She really did wish she could be good at speech.

On Open House Day, when all the children's parents
were invited to visit the school, Ally was always the one
to dress up in a sparkly leotard and dance around on
stage with a big fake lollipop and sing 'On the Good
Ship Lollipop' both with her voice and also using her
mother's stiff sign language. All the teachers and parents
crowded around her afterwards, and her picture was up
in the hall for weeks and weeks.

Ray's parents never came to the Open House Day.
Sophie would watch Ray look around anxiously for a
familiar face in the audience, never finding one. Often
he would find Joey instead and go and stand by him; he
usually had the best place in the middle of the crowd
around his older brothers, all of whom could tell stories
even better than he could. There was one particularly
great one about breaking through the layers of the world
one by one, the membrane splitting open around your
face, your face hitting the thick cold air, flying, flying,
flying to the next layer, breaking through, floating
around the stars, until finally you were outside the
whole universe, looking down at the small round ball
that was the planet Earth, rotating far away down below
you, a tiny ocean rising and falling on the small Earth.
Then a big rubber band would pull you fast back down,

down, down, so fast through all the layers, until with a big physical bang on your belly you were back where you started.

Then their teacher would come up to the group and tell Ray and Joey to go and line up now for lunch.

Once, one of the worst teachers, an old, square woman with thick glasses who could hardly sign at all, came up in the middle of one of Joey's brothers' stories and yanked Ray away. It was at the exciting part and Ray was just at the stage where he had stopped only being able to open and close his mouth during class and was starting to say more, starting to be able to ask questions and explain what he liked and didn't like.

He was still hesitant though, unsure of words and of actually making anything about himself understood to anyone else. When he lingered beside Joey in the middle of the crowd around Joey's brothers telling their stories, there was a new quality in his stare, a new hunger. He knew the taste of what it was he wanted so badly now, and where it was, but he just didn't know how to get it for himself. He was like an alcoholic watching a punter drink the first froth off a strong and hearty Guinness, or a person with a sweet tooth looking into the bakery window at the richest and darkest chocolate tart.

Sophie saw Ray hold up a finger to the teacher. Just one moment, he was saying. Just one more moment till the story ends and then I'll go in to lunch. His eyes were dark brown and intense on Joey's brother, wanting,

wanting just for the last bit of the story. His lower jaw was slightly open.

But the teacher kept shaking Ray's shoulder.

—You must come now to lunch. Look at me! Pay attention when you're told to! she said in her few words of ugly sign language, not understanding what Joey's brother was saying. She was mostly speaking, signing only the key words. Must. Come. Look. Me.

Again she shook Ray, hard.

Sophie saw Ray turn around, his eyes still on Joey's brother, and use one arm to nudge himself roughly out of the teacher's grasp.

The next day when she came to school, Joey told her that Ray had been sent home for a week because the teacher had said he shoved her.

They both knew that when he came back he would be even worse off, after a week at home not being able to communicate with anyone at all, a week not understanding how he had come so close to the chocolate tart in the window and then by some strange fate had ended up so far away from it again.

And it was like that – he *was* even worse off when he got back to school.

When she was an adult, Sophie always remembered the look in Ray's eyes that day as he watched Joey's brother and told the teacher to wait – that intense, complete hunger she knew now was something you saw so rarely in people outside of sex, or that they admitted to.

Sometimes, once in a very long while, she would go back to visit the town and the school. The town was still full of fast-food restaurants and the hills felt even more brown and ugly now that she'd seen more of the world outside. She would go to watch a basketball game and say hello to everyone she had known as a child who was still there and meet their children and grandchildren.

Ray was still there. He would often hang out in the parking lot with Joey, telling stories.

LOUISE STERN was born in 1978 and grew up in Fremont, California. She is the fourth generation of her family to be born deaf. She has lived in London since 2002.

ACKNOWLEDGEMENTS

This book is for the deaf community and for Angus.

Thank you to all the family, Oliver Pouliot, Sophie Pierozzi, Liz Jobey, Hannah Westland, Carrie Braman, Jolene Mahoney-Beaver, Beth Ebberts, Cat Cassidy, Jessica Hinman, Lana Pascall, Cara Amores, Therese Rollven, Aaron Williamson, Mark Hopkinson, Terry Giansanti, Deepa Shastri, Will and Katja, Stephanie Cobb, Jonathan Ellery and Browns, Laura Holmes, Robert Wirth and the Hassler Hotel, Sam Taylor-Wood, Shiraz Ksaiba, Steven Fisher, and Denci.